Fatal Fall

A Lori Reynolds Mystery

by

Teresa A. LaRue

For information, email **Cozy Cat Press**, cozycatpress@aol.com or visit our website at: www.cozycatpress.com

COZY CAT
P R E S S

ISBN: 978-1-946063-39-7

Printed in the United States of America

Cover design by Paula Ellenberger
www.paulaellenberger.com

1 2 3 4 5 6 7 8 9 10

For those who have shaped my life: my parents, who have always stood with me, my late husband, my one and only sibling, and my three wonderful children

CHAPTER ONE

It was late afternoon by the time Lori Reynolds exited Interstate 10 and made her way to the entrance of Oakwood Manor, along the Mississippi Gulf Coast. The urge to turn around and scurry back to the safety of her apartment in Texas was strong.

Unfortunately, flight was not an option.

Today, the wrought iron gate stood open. Before she could lose her courage, she slipped through the narrow opening and headed down the crushed shell drive. Overhead, massive oaks formed a thick canopy of leaves, which blotted out most of the remaining light, and sent shadows dancing across the hood of her car.

In the distance, she spotted the pristine, white building with its six fluted columns rising majestically in the air, and her heart began to race. For the past seven years—since she was nineteen—she'd made a point of staying away from this place and the memories it held. Usually she used work as an excuse. Other times, she begged off by saying she'd made plans to spend the holidays with friends. Any excuse to avoid the place.

Now there would be no more invitations to visit because her older sister Kay was dead. An accident, her brother-in-law, Trevor Grant, had said when he'd called with the news. But Lori knew better. Someone had pushed Kay down those stairs. And she was here, not only to bury her sister, but to find out who'd killed her and the unborn child she was carrying.

By the time she reached the house, her hands were trembling. She pulled her ten-year-old Toyota in beside a silver Lexus and shut off the motor. For a long while, she sat there, staring into space, as a wave of loneliness engulfed her. Why hadn't she spent more time with Kay when she'd had the chance? Work hadn't been *that* important. Her heartbreak over losing Marc, her best friend in the whole world, to Selena, Trevor's conniving daughter from his first marriage, shouldn't have kept her from visiting her only sister. After all, Kay had sacrificed her dream of going to graduate school after their parents had died in a car wreck to take on the task of raising her younger sister.

If only she could go back, rewind time . . . Who was she kidding? She'd probably do the same thing.

Through a blur of tears, she saw the front door open and Trevor bound down the steps. Wiping away her tears, she crawled out of the car to greet him.

From a glance, it seemed the years had been good to him. The dark blue suit he had on showed off a lean body, which she suspected, came from countless hours spent on the tennis court, not plugging away in some gym. As he drew closer, she was surprised to find his once coal-black hair threaded with gray and his dark brown eyes surrounded by a mass of wrinkles. A quick mental calculation and she remembered he would now be forty-nine.

"We weren't expecting you until tomorrow." His bushy brows knotted together to form a slash across his deeply tanned forehead.

"Yeah, well,"—Lori rubbed her aching neck—"I was too wound up to sleep, so I just kept driving. Next thing I knew, I was at the turnoff." Realizing her early arrival might present a problem, she quickly added, "I can get a room in town if it's a problem."

"Nonsense. You know you're always welcome here.

This is your home. In fact, Kay had always hoped—" he broke off, and a stab of pain shot across his face.

Lori stood by, not knowing how to comfort him, her eyes clouding with tears. She finally shuffled over and gave his shoulder a pat. To her relief, he pulled himself together and pasted on a half-hearted smile. "Where are my manners? It's really good to see you again. I'm just sorry it has to be under these circumstances."

"Me, too," she said softly. Then, hoping to erase the sadness from his eyes, added, "You're looking good."

"Thanks." That half-hearted smile was back. "Look, I know you must be tired. Why don't you go inside and relax, while I take care of your luggage. There's a pitcher of iced tea on the coffee table if you're thirsty."

Grateful for his kindness, she handed him her keys, then trotted up the front steps. As she stepped into the foyer, an irresistible force drew her toward the stairs along the left wall. A voice inside her head cried out: *This is where it happened. This is where Kay died.*

A jolt of horror slammed through her body, causing her knees to buckle. Behind her, a door opened, someone yelled, then strong arms encircled her sagging body. Then she was half-carried, half-dragged into the living room and dumped onto the sofa. A few minutes later, a glass of iced tea was forced into her hands.

At Trevor's insistence, she downed a few gulps of the sweet liquid, then placed the glass on the coffee table and leaned back. "You can quit worrying. I'm fine. I just felt a little dizzy for a minute there. My blood sugar was probably low from skipping lunch."

Trevor continued to hover beside her, a doubtful expression on his face. "Maybe I should have a doctor check you out and make sure you're all right."

Another voice chimed in: "Oh, for goodness sakes, Father. Leave the poor girl alone. She said she was fine."

She knew that voice. Over the years it had been indelibly stamped on her brain. A quick scan of the room revealed its source, next to a bank of floor-length windows.

Assured she had Lori's attention, the young woman let the drapes fall gently into place and strolled across the room to join them. Unlike her father, there was no smile of welcome on her lips.

A familiar anger began to pulse inside Lori at the sight of Selena, her old, childhood friend. They'd been raised as sisters when Kay had married Selena's father when Lori was eleven and Selena twelve, but the two girls had never been close. In fact, Selena had always been jealous of all the attention Lori got.

Now, though, as Lori looked up, she willed herself not to act on her feelings—but only for Trevor's sake. "Hello, Selena," she forced the words out. "Long time, no see."

Where Selena's copper-colored hair had once fallen to her waist, it was now cropped to chin-length in one of those deliberate messy styles that make you want to reach for a good, stiff brush. The long, narrow face seemed a bit paler, as if it hadn't seen the sun in years. But her eyes—those enormous, cat-green eyes—looked as cruel as ever.

"You seem surprised to see me," Selena said, picking a piece of lint off her brown, cotton pants. "Didn't Kay tell you that Marc and I sold our house and moved back home? It's just temporary. The move, I mean. Until we find a place that suits us." She glanced at Trevor. "How long has it been now, Father? Six, or seven months?"

"About six, I guess." He shifted from foot to foot as if he would rather be somewhere—anywhere—else at the moment.

Six months didn't sound all that temporary. "I hope

you're not having financial difficulties." Though Lori tried to keep her tone civil, it wasn't easy. She tossed out the well-used line, "In today's economy lots of people seem to be having a tough time making ends meet. Some are even losing their homes."

Selena pursed her lips. "We didn't lose our home. We sold it. There's a big difference."

Lori shrugged. "Sorry. I didn't mean to imply—"

"Actually, things couldn't be better," Selena hurried on. "Marc and I both have jobs we love. We pay our bills on time. We've even managed to put aside a little money for emergencies."

"That's good," Lori replied, with fake sincerity.

Selena eyed her speculatively. "I always figured you'd find your way back here someday. I'm just surprised it took you so long."

"Really?" Lori's voice registered skepticism. "That's funny because I never planned on coming back here. If it hadn't been for Kay's"—she nearly blurted out the word *murder*, but caught herself in time—"death, I wouldn't be here now."

"If Kay's death hadn't brought you back, you would have found some other reason to come back."

Lori's temper ratcheted up a notch. "I seriously doubt that—"

"How about some cookies to go with that tea, girls?" Trevor said, looking hopeful.

They ignored his offer.

"Face it," Selena went on, "Kay's death was just a convenient excuse for you to come home."

Realizing where this word play was headed, Lori cut short the chitchat and zeroed in on the reason behind Selena's supposition. "How is Marc these days?"

For the briefest instant, anger flared in those cat-green eyes, but was quickly snuffed out. Then Selena smiled, once again in control of her emotions. "Marc's fine. Terrific, in fact." She ambled across the room and slid into the chair across from Lori. "That reminds me. A few weeks ago we happened to be passing through your neck of the woods. Since we were so close, I told Marc we should stop by and make sure you were okay. After all, nobody's seen you in awhile."

I'll believe that story—the day alligators sprout wings and fly, thought Lori. *You weren't worried about me. You just wanted to gloat over the fact Marc was yours, not mine.*

"But"—Selena settled back against the blue-flowered cushion with that smug look on her face that Lori knew so well—"he told me he planned on turning the trip into a second honeymoon and he didn't think we'd have time, or energy, to do any visiting."

Knowing her words had struck their target, Selena was content to sit back and bask in her triumph.

Lori's blood began to sizzle. "I don't remember you taking a first honeymoon. Seems to me you were too sick to travel at the time."

"What's that supposed to mean?" There was a hard edge to Selena's voice.

Recognizing the danger signs, Trevor wedged himself between the pair. "Lori, maybe you'd like to head upstairs and get settled, maybe take a nap. Or relax in a nice, warm bubble-bath and wash the grime off."

Determined to hold her own against Selena, Lori replied, "I thought I might sit here and visit a while first. Find out what everybody's been up to. How's your grandmother doing, Selena? She still lives here, right? You haven't dragged her off to some assisted living place, have you? And where's that darling niece of mine?"

Trevor turned his attention to Selena. "I thought you had some business to take care of in your workshop.

Something about orders that needed to be filled."

"Where are your manners, Father?" Selena flicked a hand in Trevor's direction. "It would be rude of me to run off before Lori and I have a chance to catch up. Her eyes narrowed. "Now, let's discuss the *real* reason you've avoided this place."

Before the battle between the women could escalate into an all out war, a tall, well-built man wearing a tan Stetson and faded Levi's strode into the room. A shiny pair of alligator-skin boots completed the cowboy look he was going for.

In Selena's haste to greet this new arrival, Lori was quickly forgotten. "Derek!" Selena flew across the room and flung her arms around the man's neck. Questions poured out. "When did you get back? Have you had anything to eat? How was your trip?"

"Hold on, kitten." The man laughed as he removed his hat, allowing a mass of short, black hair to spring out. "One question at a time, if you don't mind," he said gently, then leaned over and planted a kiss on top of her head. "I just got back a few minutes ago, so, no, I haven't had time to eat yet. And my trip went about as well as could be expected."

Tossing his hat on a nearby table, the man bounded across the room toward Lori and held out his hand. "I'm Derek Grant." When Lori started to introduce herself, he shook his head. "No, don't tell me. You must be Lori, the long, lost sister."

When his words registered, Lori's eyes widened in surprise. She shot Trevor a questioning look. Realizing an explanation was in order, he plopped down beside her and obliged. "Derek's my younger brother by six years, which makes him forty-three now, I guess. Of course, though, we haven't seen much of him in the last twenty years, or so. He's been hopscotching around the planet. I believe he might have been in South America when you lived with us. I'm sure you must've heard us mention his name from time to time."

Lori shook her head. "I was under the impression you were an only child."

"Because Trevor prefers it that way." Derek lowered his voice to a dramatic whisper. "You see, I'm what some call the black sheep of the family. Most of the time, big brother here"—he motioned toward Trevor—"likes to pretend I don't exist."

Trevor rolled his eyes. "Which is hard to do when you're living in my house, eating my food, working beside me every day of the week."

Derek ignored his brother's comment and turned back to Lori. "While you're here, I hope we can get better acquainted. Kay talked about you so much; I feel like we're already old friends."

Squirming under his intense gaze, Lori was grateful when Selena nudged his arm and handed him a glass of iced tea.

He took a big gulp, then sighed. "Thanks, kitten. I needed something cold. I've been on the road most of the day. But I thought . . . after what happened . . . well, I'd better get home as quickly as possible."

Selena's face lit up with his thanks as if she were a puppy being praised by her master.

After a few more gulps of tea, Derek settled into one of the plush, velvet chairs that flanked the couch. And, like any well-trained pup, Selena trotted over to perch along the armrest, ready to fetch whatever her master needed.

Lori caught Trevor's frown of disapproval, and was glad he had the good sense not to voice his opinion about the matter. It was a well-known fact that Selena hated being told what to do—especially by her father.

Once again, Derek's crystal blue eyes sought Lori's. "I was beginning to think you were a figment of Kay's imagination. There was all this talk about a sister, but no sister ever turned up at any of the family gatherings."

Feeling her cheeks grow warm, Lori said, "I've been pretty busy these last few years. There hasn't been much time for vacationing."

He smiled. "Well, you're here now, and I'd like to get to know you better. For starters, I don't remember Kay mentioning what type of work you're in."

Ignoring the bolt of anger Selena slung her way, Lori said, "I'm a photographer."

"Sounds interesting. Do you specialize in any particular area?"

"Portraits mostly. Occasional weddings."

For the next few minutes, Derek bombarded her with questions about her work, her recreational activities, and her life in general. She managed to come up with enough details to satisfy him. Of course, she skipped over the part about once being in love with Marc, his niece's husband.

"Then why the move to Dallas?" He seemed genuinely puzzled. "I mean, Kay talked about how much you loved this part of the country. Especially being near the water. Not too much of that in your part of Texas."

Realizing they were gliding into dangerous waters, Trevor tried to steer the conversation away from the past. "How did the trip go, Derek? Were you able to contact all the people we agreed on?"

Derek locked eyes with Trevor. "Don't I always get what I go after?" Some underlying message seemed to pass between the brothers. "You, of all people, should know that."

"Not always," Trevor quickly replied. "Remember when you—"

Derek's jaw tightened. "I wouldn't go there if I were

you, big brother."

The air suddenly pulsed with tension. Whatever lay between the two brothers had to be more than a simple business disagreement.

"Father, why don't you and Uncle Derek discuss this later?" Selena laid a protective hand on Derek's shoulder. "He just got home. I know he'd appreciate a chance to clean up before supper. Besides, I'm sure he did the best he could in D.C."

Anger smoldered in Trevor's eyes. "'The best he could,' isn't good enough. We have a business to run. People who depend on us. If he spent half as much time working as he did playing golf, he'd know how important this contract is to us. Small shipyards like ours are going under all the time."

Derek scrambled to his feet, almost knocking Selena to the floor in the process. "How many times do I have to remind you—this was *my* father's company, too? I have a degree in business and almost twenty years experience in the field. Those two things alone should entitle me to some respect."

Trevor stood up. "Respect has to be earned."

The pair stood facing each other, neither willing to back down. "Look, I know what I'm doing," Derek finally said, ending the standoff. "You're just going to have to trust me."

"That's not easy."

Derek's eyes narrowed. "I know I screwed up last time. I shouldn't have let my temper get the best of me. Believe me, it will never happen again."

"It had better not." The vein in Trevor's temple bulged. "The only reason I didn't fire you then is because you're my brother. Believe me, if I hadn't promised Mother I'd make a place for you, you'd be history by now."

Derek's hands clenched into fists. "If you want to

fire me, go ahead. But I'll make sure everyone knows about—"

Trevor took a step forward. "You might want to consider the consequences before you go making accusations."

Selena shoved her way between the brothers. "Father, Uncle Derek is tired. I'm sure he didn't mean to upset you." When Trevor showed no sign of backing down, she pleaded softly, "Please."

Lori held her breath and waited to see if Selena's words could slice through her father's testosterone-doused brain.

With an effort, he shucked off his anger. Turning to Lori, he said, "I hope you'll forgive our bad manners. We're not usually so rude." He nodded toward Selena. "Why don't you take Lori upstairs and get her settled in the blue room. I'll be up in a few minutes with her luggage."

Selena stood there a moment, eyeing the two men, looking uncertain.

"Go ahead, kitten," Derek urged. "Do as your father says. He and I have a few more business matters to sort out, but I promise things won't get out of hand."

Abandoning her referee duties, Selena grabbed Lori's arm and ushered her toward the door. "Come one. We may as well give them some privacy. Heaven knows, there's little enough of it around here."

CHAPTER TWO

Selena was halfway up the stairs before she realized Lori wasn't behind her. With a sigh, she turned around and clumped back down. "You'll have to face them sooner, or later." She sounded so calm, so matter-of-fact, but then, it wasn't her sister who had fallen to her death here.

"Give me a minute," Lori replied, fighting to hold back tears.

The sound of raised voices exploded from the living room, causing a look of indecision to slide over Selena's face. Without conscious thought, Lori's feet started moving. "Where's this room you're supposed to take me to?" she asked. "And what's the matter with my old room? I left some of my stuff in there. I hope Kay didn't throw any of it away."

Reverting to her bossy ways, Selena muscled past Lori, turned left at the top of the stairs, and headed toward the east wing. "I've turned your old room into my sitting room," she said. "Besides, Kay put a lot of effort into decorating this room for you. She even had a bathroom installed so you wouldn't have to trot down the hallway in the middle of the night. But, of course, you never bothered to show up to appreciate all her hard work. As for your stuff, I think it's packed away in the attic somewhere."

Lori wrestled with the idea of Selena taking over her old room and concluded she didn't like the idea. After all, it was still *her* room. And though she had no plans to move back in, she liked the idea it was there if she ever needed it. If Selena needed more space, she should pack up her stuff and move into the east wing.

"I hope you're not going to be squeamish about being in this part of the house alone," Selena said, interrupting her thoughts. "Kay was in the process of redoing this section of the house. I think she'd planned on moving Uncle Derek into the room next to yours, but he decided to take over Granddaddy's old cottage instead. The place was in pretty bad shape when he moved in, but he made some repairs and seems pretty happy there."

"I'm not afraid of ghosts, if that's what you're implying."

"I was thinking more along the lines of an intruder, but ghosts roaming about the place sounds more interesting. Lots of these old houses have them, you know."

Selena led her to a room at the far end of the hall that was once used mostly for storage. She pushed open the door, then stepped back and waited for Lori to enter.

Soft rays of light streaming in from a wall of windows along the south side gave Lori a clear view of the beach and the Gulf beyond. The room itself was done in cool shades of white and blue. A queen-sized bed took up most of the space, sporting a white, quilted bedspread complete with gossamer canopy. Matching dresser and chest of drawers provided for plenty of storage.

Along the far wall, several wicker chairs with blue flowered cushions were arranged around a glass table. In its center, a huge vase of silk, fuchsia-colored azaleas provided a warm touch of color.

She wanted time to savor this last gift from her sister, but with Selena glued to her heels that was impossible. Though she threw out a few not-so-subtle hints about being tired, Selena ignored them. Then, making herself at home on the bed, she actually had the audacity to ask Lori to join her.

Spending a minute longer in Selena's company was the last thing she wanted to do. "Can we talk later? I've been on the road all day. I'd really like to rest for a while."

"You can't be that tired. I'm sure a little sisterly comfort is just what you need at the moment."

Lori was quick to set her straight. "We're not sisters."

Selena shrugged. "Your sister married my father when she was barely twenty-one. You and I grew up together. I'd say that makes us, for all practical purposes, sisters."

From past experience, Lori knew there was no use arguing with Selena, who had her own way of looking at things. It was better to save her strength for more important matters. So she trotted over to the bed, sat down, and waited for Selena to spit out what she had to say and be on her way.

Selena twisted around to sit cross-legged on the soft mattress, "Now, why don't you tell me what you've been up to out there in Texas."

Mostly, keeping my distance from you, Lori thought. *Besides, you can't really expect us to be friends after you stole the only man I'd ever loved.*

"Nothing all that interesting. Just like everyone else, I get up, go to work, come home, do chores."

"I heard you were seeing some banker guy."

Lori frowned. "I've been going out with several men. And, yes, one of them happens to be a banker. But I'm way too busy to think about having a serious relationship at the moment."

"What happened to Philip?"

How did she know about Philip? Lori tried to hide her unease. "We broke up almost a year ago."

"The way Kay talked, you two were on your way to the altar."

"Things didn't work out."

To an outsider the two women might appear to be old friends catching up on each other's lives, but to those who knew them, it was clear that trouble lay just around the corner.

Shifting the conversation away from her love life, Lori said, "How's your grandmother doing? Does she still enjoy putting puzzles together?"

"What about that other guy?" Selena went on. "The one you were engaged to before Philip? What happened to him?"

Irritated by all the questions, Lori leaped off the bed and began to wander around the room. "I don't see where my love life, or lack of one, is any of your business."

Leaning back on her elbows, Selena said, "I'm just curious about why you can't find a nice guy and settle down."

She swung around to stare at Selena. "Like you did with Marc?"

As the silence stretched between them, a speculative look flitted across Selena's face.

"You're still in love with him, aren't you?"

Lori's face grew hot. "Don't be ridiculous. What Marc and I had was nothing more than a childish infatuation." She scooted over to the sitting area and began to fiddle with the vase of azaleas. "I got over him a long time ago."

"For your sake, I hope that's true." There was a sharp edge to Selena's voice. "Because Marc and I have something special going and I don't intend to stand by and let you spoil it."

Here was the Selena Lori knew; the Selena she could deal with.

Abandoning the azaleas, she strode across the room and faced Selena. "I have no intention of spoiling anything. But, just to satisfy my curiosity, if you and Marc have such a special relationship, what makes you think I could come between you? Unless"—she paused for effect—"your relationship isn't as strong as you'd like everyone to believe."

Selena shot off the bed like a torpedo. "Don't play games with me, little sister," she warned. "I don't take hostages. I just pulverize anyone who gets in my way."

The hardness in those emerald eyes sent a chill racing up Lori's spine.

Noting her reaction, Selena smiled. "Bury your sister," she said, "then go home to Texas where you belong."

***

As soon as she was alone, Lori collapsed in the nearest chair and berated herself for letting Selena get under her skin. It wasn't like she was a naive teenager anymore. She was a grown woman. One who was perfectly capable of standing up for herself.

Instead of sitting around stewing over the matter, she leapt to her feet, strode into the bathroom, and filled the tub with warm water. After climbing in, she closed her eyes and let her mind drift off to a make believe world where everything was peaceful and she was in control of her emotions.

By the time the water cooled, she felt calmer. She dried off and walked into the bedroom. As promised, her suitcases were piled next to the bed. She chose a white blouse and navy blue skirt for tonight's event, then tried to disguise the tiredness in her caramel-brown eyes with make-up. After adding a coat of rose-colored lipstick, she ran a brush through her short, blond hair, then headed downstairs.

She made it to the foot of the stairs, before fear

paralyzed her body. How could she face Marc again? So many years had gone by. Would the connection they'd once shared still be there?

Somehow, she'd always pictured their meeting taking place under different circumstances. Perhaps, bumping into each other coming out of the theater, or standing in line for coffee. Never once had she imagined the scene unfolding in her childhood home, under Selena's watchful eyes.

Well, she couldn't stand here all night cowering by the stairs. Squaring her shoulders, she marched into the room with her head high. When she realized Marc wasn't among those gathered, the tension in her neck and shoulders slowly dissipated.

"I was about to run up and see if you'd fallen asleep," Derek said, tossing his magazine aside.

Her face grew warm. "Sorry. I didn't mean to hold everyone up." She shot Trevor, who was seated next to Selena on the sofa, an apologetic look. "I wasn't sure what time you usually had supper."

Though Trevor and Derek had on the same clothes they'd worn earlier, Selena had changed into a slinky, black dress that put Lori's modest outfit to shame.

"We normally eat around six," Trevor said, "but we're running a little late this evening because Marc got held up at work. Something about an order that didn't come in. I'm sure he'll be along shortly."

At the mention of Marc's name, Lori's heartbeat shifted into overdrive. Trying not to betray her nervousness, she slid into the empty chair beside Derek.

He took a moment to study her face. "You're looking more rested."

She rewarded him with a smile. "It's amazing what a little water therapy and makeup can do for a woman."

Selena glanced impatiently at her watch. "I hope Marc hasn't forgotten that we need to be at the Stevens' by eight."

Trevor's eyes widened. "Considering the circumstances, don't you think you should cancel your plans for the evening?"

"Are you crazy?" A vertical slash appeared between Selena's eyes. "I had to do a lot of schmoozing to get on the guest list for this party. All the movers and shakers in town will be there. No way am I going to blow this opportunity."

"I'm sure Mr. Stevens doesn't expect—"

"Get real, Father. The man doesn't care about our little problems. He's a businessman. All he cares about is the bottom line. And I fully intend to charm my way into his circle of friends."

"I'm sure if you called and explained the situation, he'd understand."

She shook her head. "Not going to happen."

"Your father has a point, kitten," Derek said gently. "I'm sure Mr. Stevens isn't expecting you to show up tonight. He might even consider it in bad taste if you did."

Ignoring both men, Selena clamped her lips together and fiddled with the contents of her purse. Trevor opened his mouth to say something, then changed his mind.

Following his brother's lead, Derek let the matter drop. Turning to Lori, he said, "I looked over some of the photos you sent Kay. You have a good eye."

With his attention focused on her, he missed the look of venom Selena threw his way.

Wondering what pictures he'd seen, Lori said, "I do okay."

"Don't let her snow you," came a voice from the doorway. "Lori's always taken great pictures. I should know; she used me as a guinea pig enough times."

At the sound of Marc's voice, a trembling began

deep inside Lori's body. As she swiveled to face him, she felt Selena's gaze latch onto her, watching . . . waiting. For what? Her to make a fool of herself?

No thanks. She'd been down that path too many times. Slapping on a low-wattage smile, she said, "Could I help it if you liked to show off for the camera?"

After a brief hesitation, Marc lumbered across the room to greet her. The boyish features she remembered were gone. In their place was a harder, more chiseled look. But the wonderful lopsided smile and soft gray eyes were still the same. "Welcome home," he said.

For a moment, time seemed to stand still. A jumble of memories tumbled through Lori's mind, drawing her back to a happier time. A time when they'd wandered along the beach for hours. Spent Saturdays at the movies. Took moonlight rides down the coast in Marc's battered, old Chevy.

Selena cleared her throat, and the memories instantly vanished.

Marc let go of Lori's hand and strode across the room to his wife's side. Leaning down, he kissed her cheek. "Sorry I'm late. I had to track down a delivery before I could leave."

"That's why you have employees," Selena informed him. "So they can hang around and take care of things for you."

Lori caught Derek studying her with a speculative look on his face. Feeling uncomfortable, she angled her body away from his penetrating gaze.

Trevor stood up. "Since Mother and Amber are dining upstairs tonight, we may as well head into the dining room." He eased around the coffee table and led the way.

Lori was happy to discover Kay's decorating phase had not extended to this part of the house. The same, solid mahogany table dominated the room, along with its ten, matching, high-backed chairs. Against the far wall an over-sized hutch still held Kay's vast collection of figurines, which seemed to have grown over the years. The only change she could detect was a new chandelier, which was twice as large, and had more sparkling crystals.

They quickly took their places around the table, with Trevor and Derek at opposite ends, Marc and Selena on one side, Lori on the other. Moments later, Lou Ann—a robust, black woman, who had worked for the family for years—came bustling out of the kitchen carrying a bowl of steaming gumbo. Spotting Lori, she smiled. "Lordy, child, you done got too skinny. Don't they feed you in Texas?"

Lori grinned. "Yeah, but their food doesn't taste near as good as yours."

Lou Ann gave her a friendly pat on the shoulder before heading back to the kitchen. Seconds later, she returned with a huge platter of French bread and an enormous fruit salad.

As they dug into their food, Marc said, "So how are things in Texas? Is Mr. Barlow keeping you busy?"

Lori shot him a look of surprise.

He smiled. "Don't look so shocked. Kay kept us informed about what was going on in your life."

"Apparently, she didn't get around to telling you that Mr. Barlow retired. Almost three months ago. Or how, thanks to a loan from the bank, I'm the new owner of Lou's Portraits. Of course, I'll be changing the name of the place as soon as I can come up with something a little more jazzy."

"Hmmm." Selena reached for a slice of bread. "Now that you're a business owner, I suppose there won't be any more putting in your eight hours and going home. You'll probably have to hang around, hustle up more business, and take care of paperwork."

Wondering where Selena was headed with all the chitchat, she said, "I really enjoy my work, so I don't mind putting in the extra hours. But I just finished senior portraits, so things are a bit slow now."

Selena grinned. "Then I guess you'd better get home and drum up more business. Got to keep that cash register singing if you want to pay off that loan."

So that was her angle. "Actually"—Lori took great pleasure in wiping that smug grin off Selena's face— "since business is slow, I was thinking about staying on here for a couple of weeks." She glanced at Trevor. "If that's okay with you."

Conflicting emotions swept across his face. "Of course," he said, recovering quickly. "Like I told you earlier, you're always welcome here."

Selena slammed her silverware down and glared at Trevor. "I don't believe this. Lori has never shown any interest in being part of this family. She never shows up for holidays, or when someone is in the hospital. Now we're supposed to open our arms and welcome her back like nothing has even happened."

"Hey, lighten up, kitten." Derek reached out to cover Selena's hand with his own. "We don't want to give Lori the impression we're a bunch of savages."

Selena snatched her hand away. "Traitor." She stood up and nodded at Marc. "We'd better get going. We don't want to be late."

Marc's eyes clouded in confusion.

Selena shook her head in disbelief. "I knew you'd forgotten." She lifted her brows. "The Stevens' party. Eight o'clock."

"I didn't forget," he said calmly. "I called this morning and made our apologies."

"You what! How could you do something so stupid? We'll never get anywhere if you go around insulting the richest man in town. Everyone who's anyone hangs out at his parties. Think of all the contacts we'll make."

"I didn't insult anybody." The muscles around his mouth tightened. "I was extremely polite. Mr. Stevens had already heard about Kay's accident and offered us his condolences. Said he hadn't expected us to show up under the circumstances, but appreciated the call."

Then Marc's eyes narrowed—always a bad sign. "Besides, going to this little get-together was your idea. I don't know why he even invited us. It's not like we move in the same circles."

Selena's chin shot up. "Do you have any idea how hard I worked to get an invitation to this party?"

Marc took a sip of water. "There'll be other parties."

Her eyes narrowed. "You can't be serious. I had to promise Evelyn Weeks that I would take her place at the church rummage sale to even get an invitation to his party. We're lucky she's a friend of Mrs. Stevens. Now, you want to throw away this opportunity because—"

"Easy, kitten." Derek shot out of his seat. "Why don't we take a walk? All this stress isn't doing that ulcer of yours any good." He grabbed Selena's arm and hustled her toward the door.

"There's nothing wrong with wanting to move up in the world." She glanced back over her shoulder at Marc. "Opportunities like this don't come along everyday. He should be grateful for all the things I'm doing to help his career, not fighting me."

"I'm sure he appreciates everything you're doing for him," Derek said. "It's just bad timing, that's all."

Once they were gone, Trevor grabbed another roll and slapped on some butter. "Sorry about that. Selena can be . . . a bit testy when she has her mind set on something. I hope you'll excuse her bad manners."

What else could she say? "Of course."

CHAPTER THREE

When they were finished eating, Trevor excused himself and hurried off to take care of some business matters. At Marc's suggestion, they took their coffee—a thick, rich blend with chicory—and moved outside to the patio.

"I'm sorry about how insensitive Selena sounded earlier," he said as they settled into yellow-cushioned chairs around a black, metal table. "I'm sure she didn't mean to—"

Lori threw up a hand to halt his apology. "Forget it. I grew up with Selena. I know better than most people how she tends to dispense with manners and blurt out what's on her mind." She paused, then added, "No matter who she offends."

"I guess she means well," he said, but didn't sound as if he believed it.

Time to switch gears. "Who is this Stevens guy Selena was talking about? I don't recognize the name."

Marc ran a hand through his sandy, brown locks. "He's one of those casino developers who moved here a few years back."

"I saw all the billboards along the interstate when I drove in. From the number of ads, there must be tons of the places."

"Way too many in my opinion. They're catering to that get-rich-quick-without-working mentality." He leaned forward. "But enough about all that. How long do you think you'll be staying?"

How long did it take to catch a killer? "I'm not sure.

A couple of weeks probably."

He laid a hand on her shoulder. "I'm sorry about what happened to Kay. I know how close you two were."

The lump in her throat made it hard to speak. "Thanks."

"We'll all miss her." He withdrew his hand. "She was the heart of this place."

His kind words punched a hole through the dam of emotions she'd held in check for the past few hours. Tears began to trickle down her cheeks, streaking her makeup, turning her nose an ugly shade of red.

Marc slid his chair over and put an arm around her shoulders. "Everything's going to be okay," he said. "I promise."

Feeling like an idiot, Lori squared her shoulders and wiped away her tears with a crumpled napkin. "Sorry about that. I don't usually fall apart so easily."

"There's nothing to be sorry about. You loved your sister. We all did." His gaze locked with hers, held, then slid away.

Abruptly, he shoved back his chair, stood up, and lumbered over to the low brick wall that surrounded the patio. Propping a foot along its rim, he began to ramble on about some planet that would be visible over the next few nights.

But Lori wasn't listening. Her brain was too scrambled with memories she had no business reliving. When his monologue slowed to a crawl, she made some excuse about needing to unpack and fled upstairs.

It was a good ten minutes before her heart quit racing and she could think clearly. One thing was certain: she needed to find her sister's killer and get home to Texas. Because, for better or worse, Marc was married to Selena now. Period. There was no place in either of their lives for speculation about what-might-have-been.

And there was no better time to get started with her mission than now. She made a few quick repairs to her face, then set off to find Trevor.

She found him, hiding out in his study. Even though the door was open, she tapped lightly on the frame and waited for permission to enter.

"I thought you'd be in bed by now." He scrambled over, took her hand, and led her toward a burgundy, serpentine-backed sofa that was nestled near a wall of overcrowded bookshelves. "You looked pretty wiped out at supper. Was everything all right in your room? Do you need more towels? Soap? Anything?"

"The room is fine." Lori fidgeted in her seat, trying to decided how to begin. "Uh . . . I wanted to talk to you about Kay," she finally managed.

Was her imagination working overtime, or did he shift away from her?

"What do you want to know?"

"When you called to tell me about Kay, you said she had fallen down the stairs. I was wondering what she was doing traipsing around the house in the middle of the night?"

"How should I know?" There was a look of wariness in his eyes. "Maybe she got the munchies and went downstairs for a snack. Doc Sanders said that even if we'd found her sooner, it wouldn't have made any difference. Her neck was broken in the fall."

She wasn't ready to accept his explanation. "When I talked to her last week, she said her doctor had put her on bed rest."

"He did." He glanced longingly toward the pile of papers on his desk. "But you know Kay. She wasn't the type to sit around and let anybody wait on her."

"I know, but I can't see her jeopardizing the life of her baby. Not after three miscarriages."

Trevor ran a hand through his hair. "Kay didn't jeopardize the life of her baby. *Our* baby," he corrected. "She just . . . fell."

A surge of anger rocketed through her. "She had no business getting out of bed. Not in her condition. If she was hungry, why didn't she send you downstairs to get her something to eat?"

The muscles around his mouth tightened. "Probably because I've been putting in a lot of hours at work these past few weeks. And to keep from waking Kay when I come in, I've been sleeping here in the office. Believe me"—his eyes pleaded with her to understand—"if I'd known this was going to happen, I would never have left her alone."

Too keyed up to sit still, he bounced to his feet and strode across the room to stare out the open window. But even the rhythmic sound of waves rolling into shore did little to calm him.

Lori wanted to let the matter go, but couldn't. Not when Kay's killer was still walking around free. "I don't understand how this happened. Kay has been up and down those stairs a million times, and she wasn't far enough along in her pregnancy to throw off her balance."

"I can't explain why this happened." Trevor's voice sounded dead, without emotion. "It just did. All we can do now is put the matter behind us and get on with our lives. It's what Kay would have wanted."

Anger churned inside her. *How dare he think Kay could be forgotten that easily!* She strode across the room to stand beside him. "What makes you so certain her death was an accident?"

As he turned to face her, a shadow of fear slid over his face. "It has to be," he said, as if trying to convince himself. "There's no other rational explanation."

"Did you know that Kay called me two days before

she died? She said someone was playing tricks on her. Late at night, she heard voices outside her door, but when she got up to check, no one was there. And someone kept taking things from her room—her diary, the locket that belonged to our mother, and even some of the things she'd bought for the baby."

"You have to understand." His gaze slid away from her. "Kay wasn't herself these past few weeks. She was so worried about losing this baby; she wasn't thinking clearly."

"Did you hear me?" Lori's voice rose a decibel. "Someone in this house was deliberately trying to scare Kay. I don't know the reason yet, but I certainly intend to find out."

He put a calming hand on her shoulder. "Sometimes the mind plays tricks on us. We see things that aren't really there."

She shook off his hand. "I'm not delusional, and neither was Kay."

He took a step back. "Look, I know you loved your sister, and you probably don't want to hear this, but the best thing you can do for Kay is to go back to Texas where you'll be safe and let me handle things."

She glared at him. "So you can go on pretending Kay's death was an accident?"

"Lori, please, just go home. I promise, I'll look into everything you've told me. If someone *was* playing tricks on Kay, I'll make sure they're caught and punished."

Much as she wanted to force him to acknowledge the truth about Kay's death, she knew by the stubborn set of his jaw that he wouldn't be swayed. The only explanation she could come up with for his strange behavior was that he was protecting someone.

Someone he cared about more than Kay?

In a defiant gesture, she jerked up her chin. "Just so

you know, I'm not leaving this place until I figure out who murdered my sister."

***

After a night of tossing and turning, Lori woke up Monday morning with a colossal headache. Figuring a walk on the beach would do her more good than a couple of aspirin, she tugged on a pair of jeans, added a flowered halter top, and headed outside.

She scurried past the giant oaks that hugged the house, burdened down with their scraggly beards of gray moss. Even though she knew the moss was actually a member of the Pineapple family, an air-breathing plant rather than a parasite, she could never quite shake the feeling that somehow the trees were crying out for their freedom.

When she reached the open, grassy area, she let out a sigh of relief. Seconds later, she plowed down the brick steps, which led to the beach, and slipped off her sandals.

This early in the day, the sand was still cool, not yet baked to a toasty warmth by the sun. Pushing back a strand of tawny gold hair, she lifted her face toward the sun and relished the feel of salt air against her face. Closing her eyes, she listened to lace-edged waves roll into shore, allowed herself to be lulled by their soothing rhythm into a peaceful place where nothing bad ever happened.

Moments later, her peace was shattered when two large hands descended on her shoulders. A scream tore from her throat that could shatter eardrums. Without conscious thought, her self-defense training kicked in. She spun around and threw up her hands, ready to pulverize the enemy into submission.

Leaping back, Marc threw up his hands and started laughing. "Whoa there, Chuck Norris. There's no need to go all Komodo dragon on me. I was just having a little harmless fun."

Bounding forward, she gave his shoulder a hard punch. "Harmless fun. You just shaved ten years off my life. I should lay you on your butt on general principal."

As Marc stood there—feet firmly planted in the sand, windswept mane forming a brown and gold frame about his face—he reminded her of the pirates who'd once roamed these shores. In fact, she could almost picture him boarding some Spanish ship loaded down with its cargo of Mexican and Central American treasures and demanding the loot for himself.

Then he grinned, and the image faded.

"Sorry. When I saw you standing there, so lost in thought, I couldn't resist the temptation. I didn't realize you'd be so jumpy."

She folded her arms across her chest and glared at him.

"Okay, so maybe some small part of me wanted to scare you. If you'd been in my place, I'm sure you would've done the same thing."

"Maybe," she admitted grudgingly.

He gave her his best smile. "Friends again?"

Was it possible to be friends with someone you'd once been so passionately in love with? She filed the subject under the think-about-it-later category. "Sure," she said. "What brings you out here so early?"

His eyes morphed into a stormy shade of gray. "Just trying to clear the cobwebs out of my head. How about you?"

"The same."

As she set off down the beach, he fell in step beside her. "You know, even though Kay and I didn't see much of each other these past few years," she said, "there's always been this special connection between us. After our mother died, she was the one who took care of me. I always thought . . . I just assumed . . .

Well, that she'd always be there."

"You're hurting now, but take my word for it, things will get easier as time goes by."

From the glazed look on his face, she suspected he wasn't thinking about Kay's death anymore. His next words confirmed it. "You should've stayed, you know."

Her steps faltered.

He grabbed her arm and pulled her around to face him.

Uncomfortable under his scrutiny, she dropped her gaze and began to make little squiggly marks in the sand with her toes. "It would've only made things worse. You know that."

"How could it have been any worse? We lost each other. If you would have stayed around we might've—"

"What?" There was such sadness in his voice, she could hardly bare it. "Gotten back together?" Her thoughts drifted to the child he and Selena had lost a month after she was born to SIDS. "We each did what we had to do," she said, refusing to dwell on what might have been.

He lifted her chin. "You're right about one thing. We each did what we had to do. But you can't turn feelings off and on like a light switch." His hand fell away. "At least, I've never been able to."

What could she say? Their lives had gone in different directions. Directions they may not have wanted, but the moment Selena had come up pregnant, spending their lives together was no longer an option.

As if by unspoken consent, they began to stroll down the beach, each wrapped in a cocoon of their own thoughts. When they came across a cypress log partially buried in the sand, she plopped down on one end.

After a moment's hesitation, he joined her.

For awhile, they were content to listen to the caw of sea gulls and the steady lap of waves against the shore.

But she had questions that needed answers. "Has it occurred to you that Kay's death might not have been an accident?"

His head jerked up in surprise. "You've got to be kidding."

"Why?"

He shook his head. "Look, I know how much losing your sister hurts, but Kay's death was an accident. No one pushed her, or tripped her. She just lost her balance and fell."

"How can you be so sure?"

He took a deep breath. "The police—"

"—don't know Kay the way I do. You know how much this baby meant to her. She'd never jeopardize its life by wandering around the house in the middle of the night. Especially not when the doctor had put her on bed rest."

"I also know how much Kay hated asking for help," he said. "Maybe she thought she could zip downstairs, grab whatever it was she wanted, then hop back in bed before anyone noticed."

She hugged her knees to her chest. "Do me a favor. Think back over the past few weeks. Did you notice anything, maybe something that seemed insignificant at the time, which might shed some light on what was going on with Kay these past few weeks?"

He was quiet for a moment. "I can't think of anything," he finally said.

She sighed in exasperation. "You can do better than that. Come on. Did Kay seem upset about anything? Or did anything out of the ordinary happen? Maybe something that interfered with her day to day pattern?"

He frowned in concentration. "Well, she did stay in her room quite a bit," he finally said. "Even before the doctor put her on bed rest. That was unusual. Normally she always whipped around the house at whirlwind speed. But I just assumed she was being cautious because of the baby."

Lori felt a tingle of excitement. "See, that's what I mean. Something that seems insignificant, but which may turn out to be an important clue. Now what else do you remember?"

A hint of suspicion clouded his steel-gray eyes. "What's with all the questions? Do you know something the rest of us don't?"

Longing to confide in someone, she began to fill him in on the details about Kay's last phone call and Trevor's strange reaction to her questions. "Kay made me promise that if something happened to her, I would look out for Amber. Why would she ask me to do that if she wasn't afraid her life was in danger?"

"Yeah, but the idea of Kay being murdered . . . Well, it sounds pretty far-fetched."

"You didn't see Trevor's reaction when I mentioned the pranks someone was playing on Kay. I'm telling you, it went way beyond upset. There was real fear in his eyes."

"I'm sure what you saw was nothing more than grief."

"It was more than that," she insisted. "Something has the man spooked."

"I think you're letting your imagination run away with you."

"Believe me, I'd like to think Kay's death was nothing more than a simple accident." She tried to keep the impatience from her voice. "Then I could go home, work on building my business, and try to put her death behind me. But I know Trevor—he's hiding something. And my gut tells me, it has something to do with Kay's death."

Marc sighed. "Look, I wasn't going to say anything. But since you're so determined to unearth all our secrets, I may as well tell you. Trevor and Kay had this big fight some days ago. The *guilt* you saw in his eyes was probably there because he never got the chance to tell her he was sorry."

"A fight." Lori mulled over this piece of information. Kay hadn't mentioned anything about a fight when she'd talked to her on the phone last Wednesday, so this must have taken place after they'd spoken. "Do you have any idea what they were arguing about?"

He shrugged. "Nothing important. Certainly nothing worth killing over."

She crossed her arms and glared at him.

"Okay." He finally caved. "Kay wanted to send Amber to summer camp, but Trevor didn't think she was old enough to be away from home that long."

"That doesn't sound like Kay. When I tried to talk her into letting Amber spend a couple of weeks with me last summer, she wouldn't hear of it. She just kept saying, 'my baby's too young to be away from home.' Now she wants to send Amber away for the whole summer. Sounds pretty suspicious to me."

"I doubt Amber would've been gone all summer," he pointed out. "Besides, there's nothing unusual about a kid going to camp. You probably went yourself."

"I was fourteen years old."

"And I'm sure it did you a world of good."

"I'm telling you," she said, "something is wrong here. If you'd seen the look on Trevor's face . . . "

"Maybe he's worried about getting caught in the crossfire between you and Selena," he said, not convinced.

Her chin jutted out. "I'm telling you; he's hiding something."

He must've realized she wasn't going to give up on the idea. "If it will make you feel any better," he said, getting to his feet, "I promise to look into the matter. Not that I expect to find anything, mind you."

She could barely conceal a smile. "That would be great."

He held up a hand. "With one condition," he added.

She waited expectantly, certain she knew what was coming. "You have to promise to quit asking so many questions. If somebody did kill Kay, and that's a big if, then I'm sure he won't hesitate to kill again. Especially if he thinks you're getting ready to expose him for Kay's death."

She crossed her arms. "Don't worry about me. I can take care of myself."

"Under normal circumstances," he said, "you probably could. But if we're dealing with a killer . . ."

Her blood pressure spiked. "Of all the pig-headed, stubborn—"

"Uh." Marc backed off. "Maybe we should head back to the house before Trevor sends out a posse to round us up."

CHAPTER FOUR

Marc and Lori trotted back to the house in silence. As they crossed the lawn, Marc let out a groan. After making a quick sweep of the area, Lori understood his reaction. Like a hawk seeking his prey, Selena was perched at one of the wrought iron tables watching their approach.

"I'm afraid things could get ugly," he warned.

"Don't worry. I've done battle with Selena before." *And have the scars to prove it*, she started to add, but caught herself in time.

Given little choice, they crossed the lawn and hoped for the best.

Despite her cocky words, Lori wasn't above trying to slip inside and leave Marc to face Selena alone. But as she veered away from the patio, Selena called out, "Don't run off, Lori. Marc and I would love to have you join us for breakfast. Wouldn't we, sweetheart?"

"Sure," Marc said, with a hint of uncertainty.

What choice did she have? If she refused the invitation, Selena would assume she had something to hide, so she changed directions and strolled over to join them. "Morning, Selena." She did her best to sound cheerful. "I hope you slept well."

"Better than you did, I'm sure," Selena said. "I don't know what Kay was thinking, putting you in the east wing alone. At least in the west wing, I'm surrounded by family. If I need help, someone's always there to lend a hand."

Lori yanked out a chair and plopped down. "Seems

to me the west wing is getting a little crowded. Maybe you should consider moving into the east wing. There's plenty of room. Unless, of course, you're planning on getting your own place soon." She sent a questioning look in Selena's direction. "Then it wouldn't be worth all the trouble of moving your things."

"We'll be moving out as soon as we find the right place, but in the meantime, moving into the east wing . . . I rather like that idea. After you go back to Texas, I might talk to Father about remodeling the rooms Kay planned to give Uncle Derek. Maybe turn them into a suite. Heavens knows, we could use the privacy. And I'm sure Marc would love his own office." She grinned. "Thanks for suggesting the idea."

"Wouldn't it make more sense to put all that energy into finding a house?"

Frown lines popped up between her brows. "That may take some time," she said. "People like us . . . well, we're used to a certain standard of living."

As long as Daddy is paying for it.

Marc snorted. "One of us is used to the finer things in life, all right," he mumbled. "The other one has to keep his nose to the grindstone to pay for it."

Selena's eyebrows shot up. "What was that, sweetheart?"

"Nothing," he said, then stuffed a piece of toast into his mouth.

While she waited for Selena to get on with . . . whatever torture she had in mind, Lori reached for the pitcher of orange juice and poured herself a glass.

She didn't have long to wait for her nemesis to get around to the purpose of this little get-together. "I hope you two had a nice chat this morning," she said, scooping up a handful of strawberries and dropping them on top of her cereal.

Marc split open a biscuit and added a glob of butter

before answering. "We chatted for a few minutes," he answered, keeping his voice low-key.

Selena smiled sweetly. A little *too* sweetly. "How wonderful." She grabbed the coffeepot and refilled her cup. "Sweetheart, we're out of cream. Could you run inside and fill up the pitcher? You know Lou Ann always makes the coffee too strong for me. Sometimes, I think she does it just to annoy me."

"She makes it that way," he said patiently, "because the rest of us like it that way."

It suddenly occurred to Lori that while Marc ran inside for cream, she'd be alone with Selena. Hoping to avoid that fate, she hopped up and said, "I'll get it. I wanted to thank Lou Ann for the meal last night anyway."

"Nonsense." Selena threw out a hand to stop her. "You're our guest. Marc will take care of it. Won't you, sweetheart?"

Marc eyed Selena suspiciously, as if trying to figure out what she was up to, then got up and headed inside.

The moment he was out of sight, Selena got down to business. "I hope you didn't get the wrong impression about anything Marc said this morning."

Lori knew better than to volunteer information. "Wrong impression about what?"

Selena took a bite of cereal before replying. "Nothing really. It's just that Marc and I have been together so long, and, like all couples, we sometimes have our little disagreements." She took a sip of her cream-less coffee. Winced. Then went on. "But the truth is: we really do love each other. Otherwise, we would never had stayed together all these years."

All this talk about her marriage—both yesterday and again today—made Lori wonder if there weren't some serious cracks in the foundation of this *perfect* marriage. She took a poke at the substructure. "What I think about your marriage isn't really important, so long as you both agree that it *is* a good marriage."

Her eyes a smoldering emerald, Selena said, "I suppose you'll just have to take my word for it."

Not in a million, zillion, years, sweetheart.

"I'm sure Marc has his own opinion about how healthy your relationship is. Why don't we ask him about it when he gets back with your cream?"

"Stay away from Marc." She jabbed her spoon in the air for emphasis. "Or I'll make you wish you'd never been born."

She was getting tired of Selena's childish threats. They weren't kids anymore. "Don't tell me what to do. It didn't work when we were teenagers, and it won't work now."

Since neither was willing to back down, they engaged in a glare-off until Marc returned with the cream. After thrusting the pitcher into Selena's hands, he sat down and poured Lori a cup of coffee, then filled his own.

Lori could feel Selena watching her every move. And despite her bold words, she had no desire to fight with Selena, so she sat quietly, concentrated on her food, and never let her gaze stray in Marc's direction.

"I suppose the vultures will be descending for the feast in a few hours," Selena finally said, breaking the silence.

"Selena," Marc spoke her name sharply.

Laughter bubbled from her mouth. "Don't bust a blood vessel. I was just trying to lighten the mood. You know how I hate all that funeral business. When my time comes, stick me in a pine box and bury me. No wake, no flowers, and no minister saying meaningless words over me."

"I'll try to remember that when the time comes," he said.

Despite her best efforts, Lori's gaze was drawn to Marc. With the early morning light caressing his face, he looked tired. Her first impulse was to reach out and comfort him. Realizing the danger in that line of thinking, she shoved back her chair and stood up. "Guess I'd better head upstairs. Make sure my dress doesn't need to be pressed."

Before she could escape, the dining room door flicked open and Annabel, Selena's grandmother, stepped outside. Unwilling to hurt the older woman's feelings, she returned to her seat.

Snow-white hair piled in a knot atop her head, Annabel smiled as she limped toward them using a silver cane for support. A soft lavender caftan floated around her plump figure as she moved. The smell of some exotic perfume wafted through the air.

She greeted them with a pleasant lilt in her voice. "Hello, everyone." As she stopped beside Lori's chair, her smile widened. "My dear, I do hope you'll forgive me for not coming downstairs last night, but I'm afraid I just wasn't up to it." She sighed. "I seem to tire so easily these days. And after what happened . . . well, I do hope you understand." She rested a frail hand on Lori's shoulder.

Touched by the kindness in the faded blue eyes, Lori covered the age-spotted hand with her own. "Of course, I understand. Please don't give it another thought."

Marc got to his feet and pulled out a chair for their new arrival. After thanking him, Annabel settled in one of the black-metal chairs, hooking her cane along the armrest. He sat back down, filled a bowl with strawberries, and handed it to the frail woman. "Selena, I'm sure your grandmother could use a cup of coffee."

His wife's only response to his request was to arch her brows and take another sip of coffee.

If Annabel was aware of her granddaughter's

rudeness, she gave no indication. "You really are a dear, Marc, but I'm perfectly capable of pouring my own coffee." To prove her point, she reached for the silver container, but Marc beat her to it. She smiled her thanks, gracefully accepting his offer.

She took a few sips of the scalding liquid, then twisted around to face Lori, turning her whole body at once, as if arthritis had fused her limbs into a solid mass. "I do hope you'll be staying with us awhile, dear. It's been so long since we've seen you. I remember how much you loved to traipse up and down the beach at all hours of the day and night."

"Don't worry, Grandmother." Selena's glance flicked from Lori to Marc. "I doubt she plans on leaving anytime soon."

To avoid a word-fight with Selena, Lori smiled sweetly, then grabbed a roll, tore off a chunk, and stuffed it into her mouth.

Selena, however, would not be sidestepped that easily. "A word of warning might be in order though. If I were you, I wouldn't go sticking your nose into matters that don't concern you." Though her words were directed at Lori, her gaze settled on Annabel. "You never know what dark secrets we Grants may be hiding."

As Selena's words sank in, Annabel's face contorted into a mask of pain. A strangled cry escaped her lips. The cup she'd been holding clattered to the table, sending a dark stain racing across the pale green tablecloth. As if she was totally unaware of the mess she'd made, Annabel heaved herself up and fumbled for her cane. Without bothering with good-byes, she set off for the house at a fast limp.

As Lori grabbed a napkin and began to blot at the rapidly spreading liquid, Marc bolted out of his chair and jerked Selena to her feet. "I don't know what that little scene was about," he said, "but I will not stand by and watch you disrespect your grandmother."

Selena tried to wiggle out of Marc's grasp, but he wouldn't let go. "That woman has been nothing but kind to us. She doesn't deserve to be treated so discourteously. Especially not by her own granddaughter." His eyes narrowed. "Am I making myself clear?"

Selena stopped struggling and met his gaze with a defiant one of her own. "I don't take orders from you. And how I treat my grandmother is none of your business."

Realizing the futility of his actions, he flung her arm aside and went to check on Annabel. Selena slumped back in her chair and began to knead her arm, where the skin was already beginning to darken. "Don't look at me like that," she said.

Lori tossed the soggy napkin onto a plate. "Like what?"

"Like I'm some kind of monster. There are things going on in this house that you know nothing about."

"Maybe so. But that doesn't give you the right to mistreat that sweet, old woman. She's your grandmother, for goodness sakes."

"And you don't think sweet, old ladies have anything to hide?"

"What's wrong with you? Anyone with eyes can see how fragile she is. What could possibly be so important that you'd risk destroying her health?"

Selena's jaw stiffened. "Let me worry about her health. As you so graciously pointed out, she is *my* grandmother."

Knowing it was useless to argue, Lori left Selena sitting at the table and headed inside. Long after she was nestled in her room, the episode between the two women lingered in her mind. What was going on between those two?

And when had Marc developed such an explosive temper? The man she remembered had always been so kind, so gentle. This new man was someone she didn't know.

Someone she wasn't sure she wanted to know.

CHAPTER FIVE

Tired of the endless questions swirling through her head, Lori scrambled off the bed and headed to Kay's bedroom looking for answers. What she hoped to find there was a mystery. If she was lucky, maybe Kay left behind some scrap of evidence that would direct her toward the person responsible for all the recent pranks. And, quite possibly, her killer.

As she stepped into the hallway that led to her sister's room, her pulse began to accelerate. Though no one was in sight, she found herself scurrying down the hallway like a frightened mouse, worried about how she would explain her presence in this part of the house if she got caught.

Since Trevor had gone off to take care of some last-minute business, she felt reasonably safe in her plundering. Even so, her hands were damp as she opened Kay's bedroom door and slipped inside. Her gaze swept over the room. When no one stepped forward to demand an explanation for her presence, she relaxed.

Before she could change her mind, she strode across the thick, rose carpet to the antique pine dresser Kay had bought at an estate sale soon after she'd married Trevor. Among the knickknacks scattered across its surface was the picture of Kay she'd taken ten years ago, during her experimental black and white phase. She picked up the picture and studied it. It was a high-key shot with soft shades of gray, which didn't begin to capture the gentleness of her sister's soul. But then, no picture could. Kay was one of those unique individuals born with a sweet, nurturing spirit that invited everyone in.

A lump formed in her throat. She placed the picture back on the dresser. More than ever, she wanted—no, needed—to find out who had killed her sister and make them pay.

Hoping that whoever had taken Kay's diary and their mother's locket had returned them, she yanked open the top drawer and began a methodical search of its contents. If she didn't come across the items, then she'd keep looking until she found them.

Heat suffused her face when she opened a drawer filled with men's boxers. But she shoved aside her embarrassment and rooted through its contents. Finding nothing of importance in the dresser, she shifted her attention to the nightstands, then the bonnet-type armoire next to the closet.

The top portion of the armoire was set up as an entertainment center. The bottom half had three good-sized drawers, two of which were crammed with DVD's. The third contained a hodgepodge of items. Among them, the red and gold scarf she'd given Kay for Christmas last year.

As she buried her face in the soft, silky folds, a faint trace of the perfume Kay always wore filled her nostrils. Caught up in happier memories, she flung the expensive fabric around her neck. As she did, something tumbled to the floor and rolled under the armoire.

She stuffed the scarf back in the drawer, bent down, and ran her hand under the edge of the armoire. Her fingers closed in on the item—a simple, gold band. She moved to the window where the light was better to study it. Too small to belong to a man, it had tiny leaves etched across the outer surface. Inside, an inscription read: *TG/JG Forever.*

JG? She searched her memory. The only name she could come up with was Jocelyn Grant, Trevor's first wife. But that didn't make any sense. What would Kay be doing with a ring that belonged to Jocelyn Grant?

A creaking floorboard alerted her that she wasn't alone. As the door creaked open, she jammed the ring into the pocket of her jeans and spun around. Moments later, a small brown head poked through. When the intruder caught sight of Lori, her chocolate-brown eyes widened, and, like a frightened fawn, she darted back into the hallway.

Hoping to calm the girl's fears, Lori called out, "You must be Amber."

The brown head popped back inside.

Keeping her voice soft, Lori introduced herself, "Hi. I'm Lori, your mother's younger sister."

Dressed like a fairy princess in lavender chiffon, the girl inched forward. "I know who you are. Mommy used to tell me stories about you." Then, with a child's bluntness, she added, "What are you doing in here?"

"Well . . . " Lori hesitated. She couldn't very well tell her niece the truth: she suspected the girl's mother had been murdered, and she was trying to catch her killer. "I guess I'm here because . . . well . . . because I miss my sister. I thought maybe I would feel closer to her here, among her things." *Not the truth exactly, but not a lie either.*

The glint of unshed tears in Amber's eyes reminded Lori how selfish she'd been to stay away all these years. If she had been a better aunt, she would've earned the right to step forward, wrap her arms around this sweet child of Kay's, and comfort her. But thanks to her own selfishness, she was nothing more than a stranger to this innocent child whose world had suddenly been turned upside down.

Though it was too late to change the past, she promised herself that she would do everything in her power to help Amber cope with the lost of her mother, just as Kay had done for her all those years ago when their own mother had died.

Seeking a distraction, Lori dug the ring out of her pocket and held it out to Amber. "I found this wrapped in one of your mother's scarves. Do you know who it belongs to?"

Before Lori realized what the girl meant to do, Amber snatched the ring from her hand. "You shouldn't be going through Mommy's things," she scolded, as if Lori were the child and she the adult. "She wouldn't like it. In fact"—she slapped her hands on her hips—"you shouldn't even be in here. I'm going to tell my daddy."

Hoping to change her niece's mind, Lori said, "You're right. I shouldn't be in here. And I definitely shouldn't be plundering through your mommy things." She sent up a quick prayer that her apology would be accepted and there would be no need to drag Trevor into this. Bending down to Amber's level, she added, "Will you forgive me?"

The small girl debated the matter for a few seconds. "All right," she said slowly, "but you have to promise never to do it again."

"Cross my heart; hope to die." Lori made a crisscross motion over her chest.

Amber grinned, revealing a gap in her front teeth.

Lori sat down on the edge of the bed, leaving room for Amber to crawl up beside her. "Maybe you can help me. I need to know where your mommy got that ring."

Chewing on her bottom lip, Amber thought about it a few seconds. "I only saw it once," she said. "When Mommy was putting it away. She said it belonged to some lady my daddy knew a long time ago, and she was keeping it for him until he could give it back."

While she mulled over the girl's answer, Amber slid off the bed and darted out the door. Lori started to go after her, then changed her mind. The girl would either keep her secret, or she wouldn't.

***

That afternoon, the funeral home was packed. As Lori stood in line with the family, people filed by to pay their respects. Some of the faces she recognized; others, she didn't.

One in particular caught her attention. Mostly, because Selena seemed so enamored by him. "Thank you so much for coming," she heard her say. "It means so much to us. Especially since we know how busy you are. And please except my apologies for not attending your party the other night."

While the man engaged in polite conversation with Selena, Lori checked him out. He had a head full of salt and pepper hair, which looked as if it had been recently trimmed. And though his body was on the short-and-stocky side, he had on an expensive suit and carried himself like a man used to giving orders and having them followed.

Lori elbowed Marc. "Who's that man Selena is talking to?" She nodded at the stranger.

"That's Mr. Stevens, from the casino. I wonder what he's doing here. It's not like he actually knows us. I think I met him once, when Selena got a couple of complimentary tickets and dragged me to one of their buffets."

A scary thought pushed its way into Lori's mind. "Selena doesn't have a gambling addiction, does she?"

"Of course not." Marc shook his head. "She just likes to hang out with the movers and shakers around town. You know, people who can help us climb the social ladder."

"I see," Lori said. "And how about you? Do you like hanging out with the movers and shakers who can help you climb the social ladder?"

He lifted a brow. "What do you think?"

"Not so much, would be my guess."

Selena led Mr. Stevens over to where they were standing. "You remember my husband, Marc." After the men shook hands, she added, "And this is my sister, Lori."

Lori opened her mouth to correct Selena, then decided not to waste her breath, since she'd probably never see the man again. "Thank you for coming." She shook the hand he held out.

"I'm sorry for your loss," Mr. Stevens said.

After chatting a few minutes, Selena hustled him toward Derek, who was propped against the wall in the corner, talking on his phone.

As Lori and Marc accepted condolences from the next person in line, her gaze strayed back to the trio in the corner. After a lengthy, somewhat heated debate, Derek extracted an envelope from his coat pocket and handed it to Mr. Stevens. Once he checked the contents, Mr. Stevens stuffed the envelope into the pocket of his jacket and strode toward the exit.

Selena said a few words to Derek, then hurried back to the receiving line and nudged her way between Lori and Marc. For the next half-hour, she played her part well—the grieving daughter, accepting condolences from friends and neighbors.

When the pastor made his way to the pulpit, signaling the service was about to start, they took their places along the front row. And though Lori agreed with the pastor—Kay was in a better place—the knowledge did little to lessen the pain she felt in the here-and-now.

CHAPTER SIX

The next morning, Lori woke up early. She slipped on a crisp cotton sundress and, tired of waiting for Marc's snooping to pay off, decided to ask a few questions of her own.

Her first opportunity to act on her decision presented itself a few minutes later. She was clumping down the stairs when a young woman carrying a dust-rag intercepted her. "If it's not too much trouble, Miss Annabel would like you to join her for breakfast in her sitting room."

Altering course, Lori followed the slender girl with her mound of frizzy, red hair back up the stairs, and to the west wing, where Annabel's quarters were located, at the end of the hall.

Since the last time she'd visited, Annabel's sitting room had gone through a metamorphosis. Gone was the elegant European luxury she remembered; in it's place was an exotic, Far Eastern motif. Bamboo print wallpaper with teal painted molding and plum carpeting, set the backdrop for facing cream-colored love seats and dark wooden tables with intricate carvings. Scattered throughout the room were delicate pieces of Chinese porcelains.

Annabel was seated at a small, round table near the window, pouring coffee. "Good morning," she called cheerfully as Lori crossed the room to join her. "I hope you slept well, my dear."

"Like a baby." Lori fudged the truth a bit.

"I do hope this will be enough food for you." She

indicated bowls of cereal, a stack of whole-wheat toast, and small glasses of orange juice.

"It's more than enough," Lori assured her, welcoming the steaming cup of coffee Annabel handed her. "I'm not really a big breakfast eater, but I do need my coffee to get started in the mornings."

Annabel regarded her with a worried frown. "I'm sure you know that most health experts agree, breakfast is the most important meal of the day."

"I would've had to be living in a cave not to have heard. Thing is, I'm usually strapped for time in the mornings. I'm lucky if I have time to grab a couple of pieces of toast, or a pop tart on my way out the door."

As Annabel poured milk over her bran flakes, she said, "Please tell me that you use whole grain bread and not that pasty, white poison they try to pass off as food, at least."

"Uh, yeah. Sure. Sometimes."

"No matter." Annabel flicked a hand in the air, foregoing the lecture. "The reason I asked you to join me for breakfast was to apologize for my rude behavior the other morning. I'm not usually so—"

Lori held up a hand to stop her. "There's really no need to apologize."

"That's very kind of you, my dear." Annabel smiled gratefully. "But there's absolutely no excuse for my behavior. Why, my poor mother would roll over in her grave if she knew how rude I'd been. She always stressed the importance of good manners, even when we were very small children."

"I'm not the only one who's suffered a loss," Lori said. "Kay has been part of your life for the past seventeen years. It's understandable if you weren't at your best."

Annabel took a sip of orange juice. "I do hope your stay here is not too boring. I wish we could have a party and invite some of your old friends, but under the circumstances . . . " her voice trailed off.

Lori cleared her throat. "I probably couldn't handle anything like that at the moment anyway. Besides, most of my friends have moved away. I didn't see any of them at Kay's funeral yesterday."

"Of course, dear. You're right." Annabel waved a hand in the air. "How thoughtless of me to even consider it. Most of Selena's friends have moved away as well. I don't know what I was thinking. I'm sure this whole experience has been absolutely dreadful for you."

Lori nodded, not trusting herself to speak.

Always the gracious hostess, Annabel quickly launched into a discussion about some book on famous gardens she found "absolutely delightful," giving Lori time to recover.

It wasn't until the meal was almost over and they were enjoying a second cup of coffee that Lori found the courage to steer the conversation in the direction she wanted. "I was wondering if you knew what was on Kay's mind these past few weeks? The last time I spoke with her she seemed pretty upset."

"Oh, dear. Was Kay upset? I hadn't noticed." The faded blue eyes looked innocent enough.

Lori leaned back in her seat. "That surprises me. You've always been so observant."

"That might have been true in the past, but as you've probably noticed, I'm not able to get around very well these days."

"Even so"—Lori wasn't willing to concede defeat—"I thought you might've sensed something odd about Kay's behavior. Something that didn't fit her usual pattern."

Annabel considered the matter. "Well, she may have been a little . . . emotional. But that was entirely understandable, considering all the hormones swirling through her system."

"She didn't seem . . . afraid of anything?"

Annabel shook her head. "Heavens, no. She'd been through childbirth before. She knew what to expect."

Lori wondered if Annabel was being deliberately obtuse. "I wasn't talking about—"

"If you don't mind a little advice from an old woman, dear," Annabel said, "you really mustn't dwell on Kay's death. It will only cause you more heartache. I've lost people over the years so, believe me, I know how hard it is. But somehow you've got to find a way to put her death behind you and get back to the business of living."

"I'm not sure I can. Kay was the only mother I remember. She was there for me when no one else was."

Annabel leaned over and patted Lori's hand. "I know, dear. But if Kay were here, I'm sure she would tell you to go outside, soak up some sunshine, and enjoy your life."

A moment passed. Then Lori said, "What if Kay's death wasn't an accident? What if someone pushed her down those stairs?"

Annabel's chin tilted up in surprise. "Now, why would anybody do that?"

Lori met her gaze. "Because she made someone mad, or found out something someone didn't want her to know."

"I don't mean to be rude, dear, but that sounds a little farfetched, don't you think? I mean, Kay was an angel. I can't think of a soul who would want to harm her."

"She must have had some enemies," Lori insisted.

Annabel pressed an age-spotted hand to her chest. "None that I can think of." She hesitated a moment before adding, "I know you loved your sister, but this kind of thinking isn't healthy. Better to dwell on all the good times you shared."

Before Lori could reply, Derek stuck his head in the doorway, "What do we have here, a hen session in progress?" Without waiting for an invitation, he sauntered inside. Leaning down, he gave his mother a light peck on the cheek, then dragged over a chair to join them.

"If I might add a piece of advice to Mother's: You should probably be a little more careful about discussing your sister's death. You never know who might be listening." Though Derek sounded pleasant enough, his eyes were like chunks of ice.

"Do let's talk about something more pleasant," Annabel said in her chirpy, bury-your-head-in-the-sand voice. "It's such a beautiful day outside. Why don't you tell us about your plans for the day, Lori."

Realizing the futility of trying to break through the wall of denial Annabel had built around herself, Lori gave in to her wishes. For the next half-hour, Annabel entertained them with non-stop chatter about the local historical society, their senior citizens' trip to the Rocky Mountains, and her plans to take up oil painting.

Just when Lori thought the old woman would never wind down, Derek pushed back his chair and stood up. "I hate to run off in the middle of such a delightful story, Mother, but I have a ton of things to take care of for Trevor. And you know how the big man gets when us peons don't hunker down and get things done." He gave his mother a peck on the cheek, then nodded toward Lori. "If you ladies will excuse me."

Watching him go, Annabel sighed. "I do love both of my sons, but somehow they always bring out the very worst in each other. I remember one time they—" She broke off, then smiled at Lori rather sheepishly.

"I'm doing it again. Living in the past. Both my sons are always scolding me about it. It's just that . . . the past is so much clearer in my memory. Things that happened yesterday, they slip right out of my mind. I suppose it's just part of getting old."

"You're not that old. Besides, I've always enjoyed your stories," Lori said. *When I'm not searching for a killer and have plenty of time to chat, that is.*

"You're very sweet, dear, but I'm sure you have better things to do on such a pleasant day than to sit here keeping an old woman company." She made a shooing motion with her hand. "Time to go outside and enjoy the sunshine."

***

On her way downstairs, Lori bumped into Marc, who was on his way up. "Just the person I was looking for," he said. "I'm on my way into town and thought you might want to tag along." From the mysterious twinkle in his eyes, she assumed there was more to his trip than running a few errands.

For half a second, she debated the wisdom of spending time alone in his company, then that curious bent, which had gotten her into trouble too many times to count, kicked in. "Sure. Just let me grab my purse."

A few minutes later, she slid into the front seat of Marc's gray Seville. "Where are we going?" she asked, enjoying the lush feel of leather upholstery against her skin.

He grinned. "You'll find out soon enough."

No amount of prodding on her part could persuade him to cough up their destination, so she finally settled back and concentrated on the flat, green landscape flashing past her window. Since the climate along this part of the coast was subtropical, there was lush growth of all kinds: magnolias, moss-laden oaks, forests of pine, not to mention all the azaleas, gardenias, and huge stretches of marsh grass along the rivers.

"I've been thinking about the question you asked me the other day," Marc said, breaking the silence, "about whether anything unusual happened before Kay's death."

Snapping to attention, Lori gave him an encouraging nod. "I'm listening."

"It could just be a coincidence, but about a month ago Selena made this big deal about taking Kay to lunch. One of those places near the casinos, I think. The only reason I even remember it is . . . well, Selena and Kay have never been exactly close."

What an understatement! Some of the tantrums Selena had thrown when she hadn't gotten her way were vividly etched in Lori's memory. To Kay's credit, she'd always managed to hold on to her patience, though Lori was never sure if it was because Kay was afraid of Selena, or she was trying to keep Trevor out of the mix.

"Naturally, Kay didn't feel up to going anywhere with all that morning sickness. This was before the doctor put her on bed rest. But you know how Selena is." A note of bitterness crept into his voice. "She'll keep on badgering a person until she gets her way." He seemed to drift away for a moment.

"And," she prodded when he didn't seem inclined to finish his thought.

He glanced her way and shrugged. "That's it. I guess things went okay, because neither of them said anything when they got home. Of course, right after that the doctor put Kay on bed rest and we didn't see much of her."

Men. They were notorious for not paying attention to details. She tried a memory nudge. "Do you remember what they talking about when Kay agreed to have lunch with her? The two of them don't have much in common."

He hesitated a moment. "Seems like they may have been talking about somebody named Joe. Josie. Something like that."

Her mind jolted back to the ring she'd found in Kay's armoire. "You sure they weren't talking about Jocelyn Grant, Trevor's first wife?"

His forehead wrinkled in thought. "Could be."

"They've been divorced for what? Something like thirty years?"

"Somewhere around that, I'd guess."

As they crossed the bridge into town, Lori tried to put the pieces together. Could there be a connection between Trevor's first wife and Kay's death? If there was, she didn't see it.

Then why did her name suddenly pop up?

All that speculation was giving her a headache. She was grateful when Marc swerved into the parking lot of a restaurant called the Silver Sands and she could set the matter aside.

Lori glanced around the empty lot. "Doesn't look like the place is open yet."

Marc opened the car door and slid out. "You're right. The place won't open for business until eleven. But since I know the owner, I think it would be okay if we went inside and had a look around."

She joined Marc, and together they trotted up the wooden ramp that ended before a pair of sturdy, cypress doors. Instead of knocking, Marc fished a set of keys from his pocket. She shook her head. "I should have guessed. This is your place, right? The restaurant you always talked about starting some day?"

He grinned. "You could say, the bank and I own it." He unlocked the door and stepped back, allowing her to enter first.

After the brightness outside, all she could make out

for the first few seconds was a mass of black specks. Then her vision cleared, and she found herself in a spacious hallway. On one side, double doors led into the restaurant area; on the other, a single door led to a small gift shop. The brass plaque above the door read: Selena's Corner.

Drawn by the display of ceramic pieces in the window, Lori walked over and stood before the clear, glass pane. At the center of the arrangement was a hors d'oeuvre tray done in a blue crab design, a creature native to these waters. Laid out beside it were: a soup dish, a gravy bowl, and a salt and pepper set, all carrying the same design. A cookbook featuring favorite Mississippi recipes completed the display.

Marc joined her at the window. "You may find this hard to believe, but Selena made all the pieces displayed there herself."

"That's amazing." Especially since the flighty girl she remembered had been too fond of parties to consider any serious work. Though, now that she thought about it, Selena had dabbled with pottery from time to time. But Lori had never realized just how talented she was.

As if he couldn't wait a moment longer, Marc grabbed her elbow and steered her toward the restaurant. Her first impression as she stepped across the threshold was of having tumbled into the ocean. Here, there, everywhere—huge tanks of marine life were scattered about so that from every table one had the soothing view of fish and water. Overhead, various tools, which were used in the fishing industry, hung from the ceiling: trawls, crab pots, oyster rakes, to name a few.

She glanced around in awe. "It's wonderful."

His smile told her how much her words had pleased him.

After a quick tour of the kitchen, he led her outside to the deck, which hung over the Pascagoula River, or the Singing River as it was called by some. Even though it was too early in the day, she knew that he, like her, was listening for that elusive sound which gave the river its name—a sound that was said to resemble a nest of swarming bees.

According to an old Indian legend, a princess from the Biloxi Indian tribe loved a young chieftain from the neighboring Pascagoula tribe. Though betrothed to a chieftain of her own people, she fled and went to live with the peaceful Pascagoula Indians.

Angered at her action, the spurned chieftain declared war. Soon outnumbered, and facing either subjection or death, the tribe chose death. With women and children leading the way, they joined hands and marched into the river, chanting until the last voice was hushed by the dark, engulfing waters. And sometimes, on a late summer evening, the sound of their voices can still be heard.

Though she had never actually heard the voices herself, whenever she was near the riverbank, she always paused a moment . . . and listened . . . for the sound of voices to rise from the depths of the river.

A few minutes later, the peace, which had enveloped them, abruptly ended when Selena came barreling through the door. Today she had on a simple, rust-colored sundress that set off the fire in her hair. "So this is where you vanished to." She glared at Marc. "I had some things I wanted you to help me bring over to the store."

The slight tightening of Marc's jaw told Lori he was not pleased by the interruption. "I asked you last night if you had anything you wanted me to drop off and you said no."

Selena rolled her eyes toward the sky. "Because last

night I didn't know I needed to drop anything off."

Marc looked skeptical. "And when I asked you again this morning, you didn't say anything about needing help." He lifted a brow. "Or am I mistaken?"

She gave him a languid smile. "I had other things on my mind this morning."

As he busied himself wiping imaginary crumbs from his shirt, a red blush spread across his face.

"Well, don't just stand there." She thrust a bundle of keys toward him. "The boxes still need to be unloaded."

He ignored them. "It will have to wait. I'm in the middle of showing Lori around. She hasn't seen the kitchen yet."

Selena gave a dismissive wave. "I'm sure Lori won't mind waiting to see the kitchen. This will only take a few minutes of your precious time."

Before snatching the keys from Selena's hand, he tossed Lori an apologetic smile, then mumbled something about not being her delivery boy and stormed off.

Figuring Selena would bustle off to supervise the unloading, Lori trekked over to one of the empty tables and plopped down. To her dismay, Selena trailed after her and said, "Since we have a few minutes, I thought we might do some catching up."

"I thought we did all that catching up stuff the other night."

Ignoring her less-than-welcoming comment, Selena asked, "Are you still living in that little apartment near the mall?"

"Yep."

"Hmmm." Selena pursed her lips and studied Lori a moment. "I thought you might have moved into the apartment over your studio."

"Mr. Barlow won't be vacating the place until next month. Besides, I'm fine where I am."

"Doesn't it seem strange?" she asked. "Him hanging around so long. Telling you how to run the place."

"Not really." Lori drummed her fingers on the table trying to come up with an excuse to cut this gab-session short. "Besides, he's moving to Sarasota, Florida, in August, when his new place gets finished."

As if sensing her prey was ready to bolt, Selena said, "I was hoping we could get together for lunch before you leave. Do that whole bonding thing. You know— like real sisters."

Lori opened her mouth to refuse. "I don't think—"

"Not today." Selena waved away her objection. "I have too much to do for the next several days. But the store's closed on Mondays. I thought we'd go then. How about it?"

What was Selena up to? Why was she so insistent on taking her to lunch?

"There's this little place in Biloxi I think you'll enjoy," Selena said, dangling another carrot in front of her.

There was no way she could refuse her offer. Not if she wanted to find out about the mysterious lunch date Selena and Kay had shared. "Sounds like fun."

Selena stood up. "Well, I guess I'd better go show Marc where to put those boxes."

Before Selena could get away, Lori called out, "I saw your gift shop on the way in."

Her interest caught, Selena spun around. "And?"

"You've done a good job."

Selena seemed surprised by the compliment. "Thanks."

"How long have you been in business?"

"A little over six months. I opened my store the same time Marc opened his restaurant." She grinned wickedly. "Two dreams under one roof. I guess it doesn't get any better than that."

"Kay never mentioned the restaurant, or gift store when I talked to her."

"That doesn't surprise me." A spark of anger flashed in those cat-green eyes. "Not about the restaurant. She had complete faith in Marc, but she never believed I could stick to anything long enough to succeed." Her eyebrows quirked up. "Then again, that was always her problem. Underestimating me."

Lori had been guilty of underestimating Selena a time or two herself. "This place you want to take me to, is it the same place you and Kay had lunch?"

Selena grinned. "What do you think?"

Lori was seriously tempted to slap that smug look right off Selena's face. With considerable effort, she reigned in her temper. "If I had to guess, I'd say, yes. Otherwise, why bother."

A glint of excitement lit Selena's eyes. "Don't you just love a good mystery?"

"Not particularly."

"Oh well." The excitement faded. "We'll leave around eleven, so be ready. You know I don't like to waste time waiting on anybody." She turned to go, hesitated, then swung back around. "It might be better if you don't mention our plans to anybody. We wouldn't want anyone to get their feelings hurt because they weren't invited."

As Selena marched off to take care of store business, Lori's unease grew. Why did Selena feel the need to keep their plans secret? Under the best of circumstances, Selena wasn't the most stable person. The wisest course of action would be to cancel their plans for lunch.

And never find out what she was up to?

Not a chance.

When Marc returned from unloading Selena's car, he finished showing Lori around the restaurant, then drove her home. "Are you okay?" he asked as he pulled to a stop by the front steps. "You've seemed kind of tense ever since Selena showed up at the restaurant."

"Just tired, that's all."

She held back telling him about Selena's invitation, since she knew he wouldn't approve, and would do his best to stop her from going.

For her own good, of course.

And that was something she would not—could not—allow.

CHAPTER SEVEN

Too keyed up to wile the afternoon away, Lori made a detour by Amber's room. It was high time she got to know this niece of hers. Besides, children were a lot more honest than adults and she might stumble across some information that would help her understand what was going on around here. Because something was definitely out of whack in this household.

In response to her knock, Amber called out, "Go away. I don't feel like talking to anybody."

Ignoring her niece's request, she cracked open the door. The girl was sprawled across the bed, her face all red and puffy from crying. She fought back the urge to wrap her arms around this frail, lonely child and comfort her as her sister had done for her so many times. But since they were practically strangers, she didn't think her gesture would be welcomed.

"I was hoping you'd show me around." She put some pep into her voice. "I haven't been here in a long time. Everything looks so different."

Amber didn't reply, so Lori added, "You'd be doing me a huge favor."

It took several minutes of coaxing before Amber finally gave in to her request. "Great," she said. "Just give me a minute to change clothes and grab my camera."

Lori hurried to her room, tugged on a pair of white shorts and pink blouse, then scooped up her camera and rushed back to collect Amber. Though her niece had on the same blue jean shorts and white eyelet blouse, she'd washed her face and gathered her long, brown hair into a ponytail.

Outside, the sun was shining brightly, the temperature hovering in the high eighties. As they crossed the lawn Amber kept glancing over her shoulder toward the house. Suddenly, the girl came to an abrupt stop. Lori didn't have time to adjust her stride and plowed right into her.

After checking to see if Amber was all right, Lori said, "Next time, how about warning me before you decide to stop and admire the scenery? I'm a lot bigger than you. I could've really hurt you when I bumped into you."

"She hates me, you know," Amber said.

Dumbfounded, Lori could only stand there and gape.

"She's watching us." Amber gestured toward the house. "I saw her at the window."

Lori turned to look back at the house. A movement at one of the upstairs windows caught her eye. From this distance, she couldn't be certain who was standing there. "Who hates you?" she asked.

"Who do you think?" Amber sounded irritable. "Selena."

The girl's answer didn't surprise her. Over the years, Selena had spied on her often enough, using the information she'd gathered to make Lori's life miserable. "Selena has always been kind of hard to get along with. If she bothers you, just ignore her. Trust me; it drives her crazy."

Amber frowned. "You don't understand. She *really* hates me. Everyone tries to pretend she doesn't, but I know better."

She felt her heart melting. "Honey, I'm sure—"

"It's because of Daddy," she said before Lori could finish her thought. "Because he loves me more than he does her."

There could be a grain of truth in what Amber was saying. Lori had often wondered about the strange relationship Selena had with her father. Of course, that wasn't something she'd admit to a seven-year-old. "I'm sure your father loves you both. It's just that . . . you're very different. And it's not always easy to—"

A flash of anger seared through those chocolate-brown eyes. "I thought you would understand." She threw Lori a disgusted look. "Since she hates you even more than she does me."

While she stood there reeling from the impact of Amber's words, the girl darted into the woods. By the time Lori recovered and started after her, Amber was long gone. Moving through the dense vegetation, she called Amber's name several times, but received no answer.

Unwilling to give up, she plowed on, confident she would cross paths with her niece eventually. A few minutes later, she stumbled across a well-used path, which she followed to a small clearing. In the center of the space, was a small, white-framed house with a large front porch.

Had this been Amber's destination?

She hurried across a patch of scraggly grass toward the house, then halted when a round of angry voices blasted through an open window. "Just see that you don't hurt her none," a deep, rather gruff voice pleaded.

"Look old man," came Derek's swift reply, "you don't give the orders around here. You take them. Is that clear?"

"That may be so, but I'm a warning you, she's been through enough. You'd best see that you don't hurt her no more. Or you'll be dealing with me."

Suddenly, the door flew open and a scrawny, old man, wearing a baseball cap and a pair of overalls, stormed out. He looked vaguely familiar. When he saw

Lori, he came to an abrupt stop and shot a look back at Derek, who was lazing in the doorway watching him. The man's gaze flicked back to Lori. He politely tipped his hat in her direction, said, "Afternoon, ma'am," then loped off toward a stand of pines near the back of the property.

Derek stepped onto the porch and closed the door behind him. "Sorry you had to hear all that. But don't get the wrong impression; the old man and I are on the same side. We just disagree on a few details."

Lori felt her face grow warm. "I'm the one who should be apologizing. I didn't mean to eavesdrop. It's just that . . . Amber ran off . . . then I found the trail . . . and I thought she might be headed this way," she finished lamely.

Derek leaned against the railing and pulled a pack of cigarettes from his shirt pocket. "You're welcome to look inside if you want." He nodded toward the house. "But I'm pretty sure we would've noticed if she was around."

"No. That's okay. She's probably at the beach by now." Lori began to back away. "If I'm not mistaken, you told your mother you were headed to the office."

He shrugged. "I was, but something came up that I needed to take care of first."

"What about incurring Trevor's wrath?"

"It won't be the first time Trevor and I have butted heads. He tossed his cigarette down and rubbed it out with his shoe. "Besides, I rather enjoy irritating him. It makes life so much more interesting." He thumped down the steps. "Why don't I walk you back to the house? Maybe we'll come across Amber along the way."

Realizing how isolated they were, so far from the house and surrounded by a forest of trees, caused a hint of unease to settle in her gut. "That's not necessary."

She inched away from him. "I have a pretty good sense of direction. I'm sure I can find my way back to the house with no trouble."

"No doubt you can," he said. "But I'd feel really bad if you ran into that moccasin I crossed paths with on my way here."

Her gaze swept over the surrounding area. "What moccasin?" Her voice came out a squeak.

"The thing was huge. Six feet long, at least."

When she saw the corners of his mouth turn up, the pounding in her heart eased back a notch. Her backbone stiffened. "I think I can manage to get back to the house just fine on my own." As if to prove her point, she whirled around and set off down the trail at a brisk pace.

Derek chuckled and hurried to catch up. "I never said you couldn't get back to the house on your own. I just thought it might be more fun if you had someone to keep you company."

Beginning to feel foolish, she slowed her pace. "Sorry. Guess I've grown used to city living. All these trees are making me nervous."

This time, he didn't bother to hold back a grin. "You're not nervous about being alone with me, I hope."

"Don't be ridiculous!" She quickly changed the subject. "Trevor said something about you living in South America. What kind of work did you do there?"

"Who said I was there to work?"

"I just assumed—"

"That's where you made your mistake," Derek said. "Never assume anything."

She came at it from a different angle. "So you were there on an extended vacation?"

"You could say that, I guess."

"I don't get it." She stopped walking and turned to

face him. "What's the big secret? Why did you leave your home and ramble around the globe like a vagabond for so many years?"

"Vagabond, huh?" He chuckled. "Sounds kind of romantic, don't you think?"

"You must've done some kind of work to pay for all this traveling?" she persisted.

"Okay," he gave in. "Truth is: I've done a bit of everything. I've worked on loading docks, hauled freight, designed and helped build boats. One time I even worked at a spa that catered to spoiled, rich women with too much time on their hands."

"That's an impressive resume. Except for the designing and building boats, how did that prepare you for your current job?"

He shook his head. "What is this—a job interview?"

She shrugged. "I was just curious. You don't have to answer if you don't want to."

"Fair enough." He thought about it a moment. "I guess you could say my current job mostly involves people skills. How to train them, motivate them, bring them around to the company's way of thinking. And you can't get any better schooling for that than working your way around the world, having to deal with all sorts of people."

They started walking again. When they reached the edge of the lawn, he laid a hand on her arm. "I hope you realize that you've upset a lot of people by staying on."

"Care to be more specific?"

"Not really," he said. "But I were you, I'd lay off the questions for awhile. They're making some people mighty uncomfortable."

Her chin jerked up in defiance. "Too bad. If they have nothing to hide—"

He lifted his hands in a placating gesture. "Look, I'm

not the enemy here. I just think it would be in your best interest to drop the detective routine. Give everyone a chance to deal with Kay's death in their own way."

"If you know something about my sister's death, then I suggest you tell me right now."

He held up his hands in a back-off gesture. "What's there to know? Kay tripped. She fell down the stairs. End of story."

She frowned. "But—"

He cut her off. "How much do you know about Trevor's past?"

Confusion clouded her brain. "Just the basic stuff. Where he was born, who his parents were, that sort of thing. Why?"

He studied her a moment. "Why don't you ask him what happened to his first wife? What made her take off all those years ago? Why no one's heard from her since?"

"Why don't you enlighten me?" she said. "You obviously know why she left, or you wouldn't have brought it up."

"Because it's not my secret to tell," he said, then strode past her toward the house as if that moccasin was hot on his trail.

CHAPTER EIGHT

As Lori ambled toward the house, she mulled over Derek's question. Why *had* Jocelyn disappeared all those years ago? So what if her marriage went south, there was still her daughter's welfare to consider. Could there be some rational explanation for her absence? Or was there another reason she never returned to claim her daughter's heart?

Hold on. Time to reel in her imagination. There was probably a perfectly good explanation for her absence. One that Trevor would gladly share if she asked him.

She was halfway across the lawn when she spotted Amber standing near the end of the pier waving at her. Changing course, she plowed toward the wooden structure, ready to demand an explanation for her niece's behavior.

The instant Lori's feet hit the pier, Amber plopped down and let her feet dangle over the water. Slowing to a crawl, Lori tried to reign in her temper. When she reached the spot where Amber was sitting, she sank down beside her niece and let her own legs dangle over the side. "That was a neat trick you pulled back there."

"Sorry." Amber gave her a sheepish grin, then brushed back a strand of hair that had come loose from her ponytail. "I know I shouldn't have run away like that. Please don't tell Daddy. He'll be mad. I'm not supposed to be wandering around in the woods by myself."

Somewhat appeased, Lori said, "I have no intention of saying anything to your dad." She paused for emphasis. "As long as you promise never to pull a stunt like that again."

Amber gaze fell. "I won't. I promise."

They sat in companionable silence for several minutes, listening to waves lap against the pilings, watching a ship chug along in the distance. Finally, Amber said, "I saw you at Grandpa's house."

"Grandpa's house," Lori repeated in surprise. Now she knew why the man had looked so familiar. She'd seen him at Kay's funeral. Only he'd been dressed in a coat and tie, and his silver hair had been neatly combed.

"Well, he's not really my grandpa," Amber explained. "He's really Selena's, but he said I could call him that, too."

Selena's grandfather. Had to be on her mother's side. Which made him Jocelyn Grant's father. Someone she definitely should get to know. "Think you could introduce me to him sometime?"

"I don't know." Amber chewed on her bottom lip. "He doesn't like strangers very much."

"Hey, I'm not a stranger," she pointed out. "I'm family."

"Maybe it would be okay then," Amber said, sounding unsure. "But I'd better ask him first."

To protect the progress they'd made, Lori backed off. "So what do you do for fun around here?"

"Walk on the beach," Amber said. "Play with my dolls. Stuff like that."

"What about spending time with friends?"

She looked away. "I don't have any."

"Surely, there must be other kids who live nearby."

"A few." The girl shrugged. "But no one wants to come here because they're afraid of Selena. They say she's a witch."

"That's ridiculous. Selena is no more a witch than I am a fairy godmother. She's hard to get along with sometimes, but she's definitely not a witch."

"It doesn't matter." Amber's lower lip trembled. "They don't really like me that much anyway."

Lori felt a deep ache in her heart for this lonely child, trapped in a house full of adults, with no best friend to share her life with, no one to tell her secrets to. How could Kay have let this happen?

They chatted a few minutes about school, and Amber's fondness for Petey, a big, yellow cat she'd befriended and talked her mother into letting her keep. Then Lori took a few shots of Amber playing tag with the waves, building a monster-sized sand castle on the beach, and generally acting silly for the camera.

Once they parted ways, Lori trudged upstairs to put away her camera. Catching sight of herself in the mirror, she stopped to give her hair a good brushing. One of the dresser drawers was ajar. She shoved it in with her knee, then headed into the bathroom to wash her hands.

While lathering her hands with soap, she noticed the bottle of bath salts she'd used the night before was on the counter, instead of on the rim of the tub where she'd left it. She quickly dried her hands and hurried back into the bedroom.

The signs were subtle: the book she'd been reading was opened to the wrong spot; the bedspread was slightly rumpled, as if someone had slid a hand under the mattress searching for hidden treasure; and her suitcases had been shoved further back in the closet.

But there was no doubt in her mind—while she was outside playing with her niece, someone had searched her room.

The sense of violation sent her blood pressure soaring. Adrenaline surged through her body making her want to pound something. She stormed to the door, jerked it open, and peered down the hallway.

Of course, it was a waste of time. Whoever had searched her room was long gone.

After giving the door a loud slam, she marched across the room and launched herself onto the bed. When the anger faded, her first thought was, who could have done this?

Her next, why would anyone bother? She'd only brought a handful of jewelry with her. And, as far as she could tell, none of it was missing.

It didn't make any sense.

Unless someone wanted to send her a message. You're vulnerable. Alone, in this part of the house where no one would hear your cry for help. An easy target for anyone who wanted to harm you.

Was this how Kay felt when her trust had been violated?

Refusing to give in to fear, she revised her plans. Instead of waiting for Amber to introduce her to her honorary grandfather, she decided to call on him herself.

Ten minutes later, she was standing on his front porch. No one answered her rap on the door, so she tried the doorknob and found it unlocked. "Anybody home?" she called as she stepped inside.

Silence greeted her.

She stood there a moment, debating whether she should wait on the porch, or come back another time. The memory of how upset the old man was after his encounter with Derek flashed through her mind. She decided to look around and make sure he hadn't suffered any adverse effects from their argument.

There was enough light seeping through the thin, white curtains to see well enough without turning on any lights. Most of the furnishings weren't much to look at anyway. Early American castoffs, mostly. The sofa, a rusty plaid, was worn through in several spots. A solid green recliner, in slightly better condition, sat near the window. Beside it, on the scarred oak table, was a well-thumbed TV guide; a large, leaf-shaped ashtray; and a couple of photographs in one of those cheap metal frames that fold in half.

Her interest in photography drew her straight to the photos. She grabbed the picture and moved to the window, where the light was better, to study it. Both shots were clearly taken by an amateur, someone with little eye for composition. On the left was a black-and-white shot of a teenage girl standing beside a tall, dark-headed man. Judging from the clothing they had on, she guessed it had been taken in the early sixties. On the right, was a color shot of the same girl. In this shot the girl was older, early twenties maybe, with a baby cradled in her arms.

Caught up in her artistic appraisal, she failed to hear the door open until it was too late. The deep, rather gruff voice she'd heard that morning said, "I reckon you've got a mighty good reason for walking into a man's house uninvited."

Lori let out a startled whelp, then wheeled around, clutching the photo to her chest.

Amber's pseudo-grandfather stood in the doorway, the space between his eyes puckered in annoyance. Under his left arm, he carried a stainless steel thermos, while his right hand was occupied with a battered green tackle box. "I ain't aiming to murder you, so you can wipe that look off your face."

Lori's gaze shifted to the gun rack on the dining room wall, which held a couple of scary looking rifles. "I never thought you would." Without conscious thought, she shifted into her I'm-a-big-girl-and-I-know-karate stance.

He lifted one corner of his mouth. "You sure about that?"

Once the adrenaline surge abated, she plunked the picture frame back on the table. "I didn't hear you come in. You just caught me by surprise, that's all."

He cocked his head to one side. "Maybe you'd care to explain what you're doing in my house."

"Yes, well." She stumbled over her words. "Amber was planning to bring me by for a visit. To introduce us. But she got busy doing other things and . . . " She pulled herself together and stuck out her hand. "Please accept my apology for barging into your house. I'm Lori Reynolds, Kay's younger sister."

His spiky gray brows knotted together as he shifted the tackle box to his left hand. Before taking her hand, he swiped his own across the leg of his baggy overalls. "Seth Taylor."

The man's grip was bone-achingly firm. The stench of fish wafted toward her nostrils, turning her stomach a bit queasy.

"I wasn't expecting company." He let go of her hand. "But seeing as how you've already made yourself at home, I reckon you might as well stay and visit awhile."

He deposited his tackle box and thermos beside the recliner, then motioned toward the sofa. "While I wash up, you might as well have a seat." As he clumped off toward the bathroom, he added, "There's coffee in the thermos if you want some. Cups are in the cabinet to the left of the sink."

"I'm fine." Determined not to be caught snooping a second time, she trotted to the sofa and sat down, then folded her hands neatly in her lap.

Seth was back in a few minutes, smelling a lot less like fish. "Now what can I do for you?" he asked, settling into his recliner and reaching for his pipe.

Now that the moment had come, she was suddenly at a loss for words. "I just wanted to . . . I thought we should . . . "

While he waited for her explanation, he plucked a bag of cherry-flavored tobacco out of his shirt pocket and began to pack his pipe. "If you've got something to say girl, just spit it out. I know you didn't drop by here to admire my pictures, much as they mean to me."

Knowing she deserved the reprimand made her task of beginning all the more difficult. "I wanted to speak to you about your daughter." The words finally tumbled from her mouth. "I was wondering what happened to her."

"What business is it of yours?" His voice had a steel edge.

"I know the divorce must've been hard on everyone," she said, feeling as if she were tiptoeing through a minefield, "but to disappear like that. Leave her daughter behind. Why would a mother do something like that?"

"Divorce." He practically spit out the word. "You think that's what my baby wanted? That she wanted to leave her baby behind for some other woman to raise?"

The anger behind his words sent her backtracking. "I just assumed . . . "

"That man has a lot to answer for." He stabbed the air with his pipe for emphasis. "Just because he did a few good things, don't make up for all the bad things he's done."

Suddenly restless, he scrambled to his feet and strode across the room. For a long moment, he stared out the window, pipe clamped between his teeth. "It was that husband of hers," he finally said. "He's the reason my baby girl had to leave." A world of hate and pain colored his voice.

Lori felt a need to defend her brother-in-law. "I'm sure Trevor would never—"

Seth whirled around. "Don't fool yourself. Trevor

would've done whatever it took to get rid of her. Especially when he found out about—" His words died out abruptly.

"Found out about what?" Lori prodded.

He shook his head. "Never mind. What's done is done. All that matters now is that grandbaby of mine. It breaks my heart that she's grown up not knowing her mother. Everyone knows a girl needs her mother. I don't reckon I'll ever be able to forgive him for that." His anger spent, he seemed to shrivel up like a dried-up stalk of corn. He shuffled back to his recliner and slumped down.

"If you don't mind my asking," Lori said gently, "where has your daughter been all these years? I'm sure she must've wanted to see her daughter, find out how she was doing."

For a moment, it seemed as though he wasn't going to answer. Then the words tore from his throat, "In hell. That's where my baby's been all these years."

Looking exhausted, he fell back in his seat and closed his eyes. Color drained from his face, leaving it a pasty white. Lori scooted forward in her seat, ready to dial 911 if he went into cardiac arrest, but, thankfully, his breathing remained steady and his color slowly returned.

Afraid to upset him any further, she padded across the room and quietly let herself out the door.

What she'd learned from Seth had not given her the answers she sought, only stirred up more questions. But one thing was clear, she needed to find out more about Jocelyn Grant. Where she'd been hiding all these years. What she'd done to stir up Trevor's anger. And why she'd been banished from Selena's life.

She pondered the matter as she strolled along the path to the beach. It was only after she emerged from the shelter of the trees that she realized how dark the sky had grown. A stiff wind had also kicked up, causing the water to churn.

Advancing to the water's edge, she felt a raw surge of energy course through her body, which left her feeling powerful. Invincible. Like she could take on the world.

She knew the high she felt was only an illusion, created by her mind to escape reality. But she wanted to hold on to the moment. Savor it. Before life dragged her back into the real world, where life was fragile. People died. And there was a good chance she was setting herself up as the killer's next target.

CHAPTER NINE

Clad in her favorite dress, a ruffled chiffon in daffodil yellow, Lori hustled downstairs that evening, hoping to catch Marc alone. She found him buried beneath the folds of the paper. Unfortunately, Selena, a sultry witch dressed in black from head to toe, sat across from him on the sofa, sipping a cup of green tea. Derek was sprawled beside her, hanging on to her every word, as if she had blinded him with a "notice me" spell.

"How's our beautiful house guest this evening?" Derek asked, once Selena had run out of words. "Been doing any more sleuthing?"

Selena chuckled. "You'd think by now you would've outgrown your fascination with Nancy Drew. It certainly got you into enough trouble growing up." She placed her cup on the coffee table. "Remember the time you thought Mr. Sweeney had a body hidden in his freezer?"

Marc peered at Lori over the top of his paper.

"It was an honest mistake. How was I supposed to know he was getting ready to roast a pig for the fourth of July."

"Or the time you nearly gave Mrs. Jordan a heart attack when you sneaked into her house."

"I thought she was being robbed. There were two strange looking men hanging around her backyard."

"Or the time—"

Marc tossed his paper aside. "I think you've made your point."

Selena threw him a withering look. "If I'd wanted your opinion, I would've asked for it."

Derek quickly intervened. "Marc, I thought you'd be down at your restaurant this evening, making sure everything was running smoothly."

"I should be," he said, "but I thought Trevor would appreciate us all being here for supper. Besides, I have a good manager. He'll give me a call if he runs into any problems."

Lori's gaze rested on Marc. He was looking especially handsome in his white shirt and pearl gray pants, except for those dark circles under his eyes. "You look tired," she blurted out.

"Because snooping is hard work," Selena said. "All that running around, poking your nose into other people's business takes lots of energy."

"You ought to know." Marc's gray eyes were like steel. "Luis told me he caught you snooping around my office last week."

Selena's eyes narrowed. "Did he?"

Their gazes locked. "I hope you found what you were looking for."

Hoping to cut short the marital battle, which seemed to be brewing, Lori said, "I had a very nice visit with your grandfather this afternoon, Selena."

The slight flicker of her eyelids told Lori she'd caught Selena by surprise. "Who told you he was my grandfather?"

Lori hesitated. She didn't want Selena taking her anger out on Amber, nor did she want Derek to think she'd been checking up on him. Especially since the conversation she'd overheard between the two men earlier in the day had been so heated. "It was just a guess."

The look on Selena's face hovered somewhere between fury and disbelief.

"I'm afraid Selena and her grandfather aren't on speaking terms at the moment," Derek said.

Marc lifted a brow. "That's putting it rather mildly, don't you think?"

"Quit exaggerating." Selena rolled her eyes toward the ceiling. "I just don't like being around the old coot. He gives me the creeps. The man's always watching me, like he's waiting for something terrible to happen."

Lori's curiosity bumped into high gear. "I don't remember any house in those woods. How long has it been there?"

"Around two years, I'd guess," Marc answered. "Seth went through some hard times a while back. Had a lot of medical bills. Lost his home. Was even living in a shelter for a time. When Trevor found out, he had the house built and offered him the place rent free."

Derek wandered over to the window. "A big mistake if you ask me. Now he'll never get rid of the old goat."

"What old goat are you referring to?" Trevor asked as he entered the room.

"You know who I'm talking about." Derek turned to face his brother. "One day you'll be sorry you didn't listen to me. Everyone knows the old man's unstable."

Trevor's eyes narrowed. "I've seen no evidence of that."

"For goodness sakes, the man is stalking your daughter," Derek said. "If that isn't unstable, I don't know what is. No telling what's going on in that mind of his. He could snap any day and drag us into some psycho-nightmare."

"The man's seventy-nine years old. And, as far as I know, he hasn't said two words to Selena." Trevor looked to his daughter for conformation.

She gave him a grudging nod.

"The moment he becomes a problem," he told Selena, "let me know and I'll speak to him. Now"—he glanced around—"since we're all here, we may as well head into the dining room. Mother isn't feeling well, so she and Amber are eating upstairs again this evening."

While they ate, Lori studied the faces that surrounded her. Which one had searched her room? None of her jewelry was missing, so whoever did it just probably hoped to frighten her away.

Only that wasn't going to happen, because she wasn't leaving until she found Kay's killer and made sure he was locked behind bars for the rest of his life.

Lori took a deep breath, then glanced across the table at Selena. "My bath salt wasn't by the tub where I left it last night. Did you borrow it?"

"No, Nancy Drew, I did not," Selena replied. "I have my own bath salt; I don't need yours."

Lori's gaze swept around the table. "Don't look at me," Derek said. "I don't go in for that flowery stuff. If I sprain something, I soak it in plain old Epson salt, like a real man."

"How do you know my bath salt smells like flowers?" Lori asked.

"Because," Selena answered for him, "Kay bought it. Of course, it smells like flowers. That's why I buy my own. I'm not the sweet, flowery type, either. I'm into more exotic smells. Something that says—mystery and romance."

"Or that you've just stepped into a bordello," Marc mumbled.

"If you don't like the bath salt Kay chose," Trevor said, "we can always replace it."

"It's not that." Lori debated the wisdom of saying more, then decided to take the plunge, "The only reason I brought it up was because I realized someone had been plundering through my room this morning. Looking for what, I have no idea."

For a moment, the silence was so complete you

could hear an eyelash flutter.

Then Selena let out a snort. "You're not having one of your Nancy Drew episodes again, are you? Because"—she glanced around the table—"nobody thinks it's funny."

"I'm not having—" Lori began.

Trevor cut short her explanation. "The housekeeper probably moved it when she cleaned your room this morning. I'll remind her to be more careful next time." He pushed away his plate. "Now, who's ready for desert?"

***

After supper, Lori escaped to her room, claiming a headache. For awhile, she tried to settle down with a book, then realized she was too restless to concentrate on the words. Giving up, she climbed into bed and spent several hours tossing and turning before she finally fell asleep.

Only to dream of being stalked by a wild animal. She ran through the forest, shoving aside branches, never slowing down . . . until she reached the edge of a cliff. Where she faced two choices: stand her ground and risk being torn apart, or jump into thin air and fall to her death. With death only moments away, she leaped through the air like a gazelle.

And woke up seconds before she hit bottom, covered in sweat.

Once her heart returned to its normal rhythm, she rolled to her side and caught a whiff of cigarette smoke. Barely breathing, she froze in place and listened, let her gaze travel slowly over the room, searching for the predator who'd invaded her territory.

"You awake?" A familiar voice came from the sitting area.

Irritated, Lori reached over and snapped on the lamp. "What are you doing here?" she demanded.

The lamp's warm glow revealed a long-legged figure sprawled in one of the wicker chairs near the window. Leaning over, Derek snubbed out his cigarette in an empty candy dish. "I knew that if I sat here long enough you'd eventually wake up. From all the racket you were making, you must have been having a crazy nightmare. I started to wake you up, but didn't want to get my eyes scratched out."

"How did you get in here?" She grabbed her robe from the end of the bed and slipped it on. "I know that I locked my door before I went to sleep."

He held up a small, flat-headed screwdriver. "A flick of the wrist and you're in."

She marched over and held out her hand. He relinquished the tool without protest. "Now," she said, "how about telling me what you're doing in my bedroom at this hour of the night. You have to realize how inappropriate it is."

He sat up straighter. "You can rest easy; I have no designs on your body. What I do have is information. But I suppose we can talk in the morning." He hesitated a moment, waiting to see if he'd aroused her curiosity.

"Fine. I'll see you in the morning."

He lifted a brow. "Are you sure you don't want to hear this now?"

She glared at him. "Positive."

"Okay." He stood up and headed toward the door. "I just thought, since you made such a big deal about someone searching your room, you'd want to know who I saw outside your door this morning."

"Wait. Did you really see someone outside my room this morning?" Her suspicious nature took over. "Or, are you playing some kind of game?"

"Oh, for heaven's sakes. If you want to hear about this, then say so. I have better things to do with my time."

A moment passed. "I'm listening."

He leaned against the door jam. "After our little chat this morning, I came inside to pick up a few things before I left for the office. That's when I saw someone coming out of your room." He lifted a brow, waiting for her to ask.

She wasn't sure she could trust him, but obliged. "And who might that be?"

He gave her a sly smile. "None other than the big honcho himself."

"Trevor?" Her voice registered surprise. "But he was supposed to be at work."

"Maybe he had some business to take care of at home." He paused a moment, giving her time to process the information, then added, "He tried to give me this big song and dance about checking on your plans for the day. But, of course, we both know that was a lie. You were nowhere near your room."

What could Trevor possibly hope to find in her room? Her mind suddenly scooted in another direction. "What were *you* doing outside my room?"

He pushed away from the wall. "Tell me, Miss Reynolds, what does a person have to do to get on your good side?"

She ignored the question. "Tell me, Mr. Grant, what kind of grudge do you have against your brother?"

Those blue eyes turned to ice.

Realizing she might have gone too far, she took a step back.

"You're right about one thing," he said, without the slightest trace of warmth in his voice, "Trevor and I aren't close. Never have been. Probably never will be."

Lori's flee response racketed down a notch when he made no attempt to close the gap between them. "You're brothers," she said. "Sure, you may argue from time to time, all siblings do, but underneath all the grumbling, I'm sure you really care about each other."

"Right." His jaw tightened. "Everyone thinks Trevor's so wonderful—so perfect. He was always the responsible son. I, on the other hand, got stuck with the black sheep label almost from the beginning. The big screw-up. And as far as our old man was concerned, nothing but a nuisance."

Lori sensed the pain behind the words. "I'm sorry. It must've been hard growing up under Trevor's shadow."

"Don't feel sorry for me," Derek said, bouncing back to his arrogant self. "I'm a survivor. I always managed to figure out how to turn things to my advantage."

"No matter who you hurt?"

Nostrils flaring, Derek took a step toward her. When it dawned on her, she was alone with a man who could be a cold-blooded killer, her blood pressure spiked. She sucked in a gulp of air. And another. And another.

He laid a hand on her shoulder. "Calm down. Don't you think, if I wanted to hurt you, I would've done it while you were sleeping?"

Good point.

Her breathing slowly returned to normal. Once she was able to speak again, she said, "Next time you have something to tell me, how about doing it downstairs. In full daylight."

He gave her a sly grin. "What, no more secret rendezvous in the middle of the night. Where's the fun in that?"

She folded her arms across her chest and glared at him.

"I can do daytime," he said. And backed away.

CHAPTER TEN

Determined to find out what progress Marc had made in their search for a killer, Lori drove into town. Within minutes of entering his restaurant, she found herself seated at one of the dark, round tables in the dining room across from Marc. As if by magic, two monster-sized seafood platters appeared. There was no way she could eat that much food in one sitting, though Marc seemed up to the task.

She smothered a piece of fried flounder in ketchup and stuffed it into her mouth. No way was she going to count calories today. If she did, she'd be forced to consume carrot sticks and celery for the next three months.

She'd hardly put a dent in her meal, when Marc tossed the last shrimp tail on his plate and sighed. "I can't eat another bite."

She pushed her plate away. "Me either."

"But you hardly touched your food."

"Who are you kidding?" she said. "I ate like a pig."

"Is that what all that oinking was about."

"Fun . . . ny."

After assuring him for the tenth time how wonderful the food was, she followed him back to his office. As he settled behind his desk, she dropped into one of the burgundy cushioned chairs facing him.

They made small talk for a few minutes before she brought the conversation around to her visit with Seth. He listened without interrupting. "He seems to blame Trevor for keeping Selena and her mother apart." His lack of response made her suspect that her *big revelation* came as no surprise to him. "Of course, you already know this," she finished by saying.

He gave her a sheepish grin. "Seth and I discussed the matter several weeks ago when I confronted him about following Selena around."

She arched her brows, hurt by his lack of trust. "And you didn't bother to tell me because . . . "

"Because I promised Seth I'd keep my mouth shut. Besides, how was I supposed to know you were going to visit him yesterday. If you'd bothered to clue me in, I would've warned you to stay away from his place."

"Afraid I might find out what's going on around here?"

"In case you've forgotten"—Marc leaned forward—"you're the only one who believes Kay's death wasn't an accident. As far as Seth goes, I don't think you should visit him alone because he seems pretty unstable."

Seth might be a little eccentric, but unstable—she had a hard time believing it. "And you came to that conclusion how?"

Marc plucked a glass paperweight from his desk and began to rub his fingers across its surface as if searching for answers. "For one thing," he began slowly, "he hangs around the edge of the woods a lot watching Selena. At first, I thought he was trying to muster the courage to talk to her. That he wanted to get to know her, but was afraid of being rebuffed. Which, knowing Selena, was highly likely."

"That doesn't make him unstable."

"No, it doesn't," Marc admitted. "But, all the same, I decided to keep my eye on him. That's when I realized I had it all wrong. He wasn't mustering the courage to talk to Selena; he was trying to protect her."

"From whom?"

He shrugged. "Who knows? Imaginary villains. Aliens. Your guess is as good as mine."

"You didn't ask him?"

"Of course I did." He dumped the paperweight back on his desk. "Several times, in fact. But he just clammed up and stalked off each time."

"Do you think Selena could really be in danger?"

He broke eye contact. "As far as I know, Seth's never laid a hand on her."

Lori chewed on her thoughts a moment. "If Selena mentioned his behavior to Kay, maybe she decided to confront him."

He shook his head. "I doubt it. These past few months Kay's world didn't extend past the baby she was carrying."

Bursting with untamed energy, Lori hopped up and began to pace about the room, much as Seth had done the day before. Marc came around the desk and caught her hand. "I'm beginning to worry about you. This obsession with Kay's death is wearing you out. You've got to let it go. There's no evidence her death was anything but an accident. If the police had the slightest doubt, they wouldn't have closed the case. After all, they're trained investigators."

"And they're never wrong." Her voice was filled with skepticism.

"Sometimes, I guess," he admitted. "But I'm sure they're right more times than they're wrong. And, face it, there's no evidence anyone was around when she fell."

"If someone had bothered to clue them in on all the strange things going on around here, they might have dug a little deeper into her death."

"Like I said, there's no evidence—"

"I don't care about evidence," she broke in. "I know in my gut that Kay was murdered."

"The police can't arrest anyone based on your gut." He reached for her hand. "Lori, you have to let this go."

"I can't." She pulled away from his grasp. "Not until I've done everything I can to get to the bottom of this. I owe Kay that much."

Realizing there was nothing he could do to change her mind, he let out a sigh. "Then at least stick to our agreement. No wandering off on your own." He ran a hand through his sandy brown hair. "I don't know what I'd do if . . . " his voice faltered.

Without thinking, she laid a hand on his arm. Emotions she thought long buried surged to life. It was all she could do not to slip into his arms, forget everything, but the feel of his lips on hers and his strong arms around her.

His eyes told her he was caught up in the same fantasy.

A tap on the door jolted them back to reality. He bounded over to his desk and began to rifle through the stack of papers in his in-box, while she scrambled in the opposite direction, grabbed a text on restaurant management from the bookshelf, and flipped it open. The blood pounding through her temples made it impossible to focus on the words. Fortunately, she realized the text was upside down in time to correct her mistake.

Seconds later, a chunky, middle-aged woman stuck her head in the door. "I hate to disturb you, Mr. Towell, but there's a woman in the dining room who insists on speaking with you."

"I wasn't expecting anyone." Marc looked puzzled. "Did you happen to get her name?"

"Yeah, it's Mrs. Grant. Not your Mrs. Grant... Towell, I mean," she added quickly. "Though, I have to say, she does favor your wife."

His eyes widened. "Are you sure about the name?"

"Well, I didn't ask for ID, but that's what she said it was." Her brows knotted in concern. "Should I tell her you're busy?"

"No," he replied. "That's okay. Show her to a table and tell her I'll be out in a minute."

Having no idea the bombshell she'd delivered, the waitress quietly shut the door and went back to work.

Marc looked at Lori. "You think the woman could be Selena's mother?"

She tossed her book aside. "How should I know? Until yesterday I had no clue the woman was anywhere near here. Now I find out that she's in *your* restaurant wanting to meet with *you*."

"Believe me, I'm as dumbfounded as you are."

For some crazy reason, she believed him. "There's only one way to find out who she is."

He offered to let her tag along, but she declined, worried her presence might cause the woman to clam up and they would never find out why she was here. But just because she turned down his offer, didn't mean she was an idiot. After he left, she counted to thirty, then followed him into the dining room.

Since the lunch rush was over, she had her choice of tables. She selected one close enough to overhear their conversation, but far enough away so she wouldn't intrude. Thankfully, Marc was facing the opposite direction and didn't notice her.

From where she sat, Lori was able to see Jocelyn's face. There was no mistaking the aristocratic nose; the pale, white skin; or the copper-colored hair knotted together in a long French braid. This was definitely the woman from the picture on Seth's table. An older version of Selena.

Just her luck, the busboy chose that moment to clear the tables around her. With all the racket he was making, she wasn't able to make out more than a few words they were saying. She thought about offering him a twenty to take a break, but decided that might draw unwanted attention.

It wasn't long until Jocelyn completed her business. She stood up, and Marc followed suit. He waited until she disappeared from sight, then swung around and saw Lori seated nearby. "I should've known you wouldn't stay put." He strode across the room and slumped down in one of the empty chairs. His gray eyes looked troubled.

"Well, what did she want?" Lori asked.

His eyebrows shot up. "What, you didn't get an earful already?"

"Not with that stupid busboy making enough noise to rattle the dead."

"I suppose it won't be a secret for long." He paused, as if gathering his courage, then the words spewed from his mouth, "Her highness plans on gracing us with her presence at Oakwood this evening."

"What!" For a moment, she thought her hearing must be fouled up. "She can't do that. What will . . . how will . . . "

"My thoughts exactly." He raked a hand through a mass of sun-kissed locks. "I tried to make her understand that showing up at the house after all these years with no contact might not be the best idea, but she didn't seem to care."

"That's an understatement if I ever heard one. It's not every day a woman nobody has seen in thirty years returns from . . . wherever she's been." She propped her elbows on the table and rested her chin in her hands. "Did she say where she's been, or what she's been doing all these years?"

He shook his head. "She told me it wasn't important. The only thing that mattered was seeing her daughter again."

She pursed her lips. "She has to realize she might not be welcomed with open arms."

"No joke."

"Think Selena knows her mother is in town?"

He straightened. "A few days ago, I would've sworn Selena didn't have a clue. But after the way she lashed out at her grandmother the other morning, and all this talk about a Grant family secret, I have to wonder if she's known where her mother's been for quite some time."

Lori scanned through her memory. "I don't remember Kay ever mentioning Jocelyn. For that matter, I don't remember seeing her picture in any of the family albums. Which, now that I think about it, does seem a little strange—considering that she's Selena's mother."

"Now that you mention it, I don't think I've ever seen a picture of her either."

She told him about the picture she'd seen in Seth's cottage and the ring she'd found among Kay's things.

When she finished, he said, "Let's pray Jocelyn's whereabouts for the past thirty years is the only secret they're hiding."

She studied his face closely. "It seems a little weird that Jocelyn would show up at your restaurant out of the blue like this."

"Haven't you figured that out by now?" He crossed his arms. "I'm her John the Baptist, given the task of preparing the way for her coming."

"Well, let's hope you don't end up like him—with your head on a platter."

"Amen to that."

She fiddled with the salt-and-pepper shakers. "Did Seth ever mention why Jocelyn fell off the radar? Seems like, even if she didn't have feelings for Trevor anymore, she'd want to stay around and fight for custody of Selena."

"Nope. He said it was none of my business."

"Yeah, that's the same reaction I got."

"Here's the thing," Marc said, doing his own rendition of the salt-and-pepper shaker dance. "Selena would never talk about her mother. Whenever I brought up the subject, she'd go into a funk that would last for days. After awhile, I decided it was best to leave the subject alone."

"Some of the kids at school used to tease Selena about her mother running off," Lori said. "When I asked Kay what happened to Selena's mother, she didn't want to talk about it. Now, I wonder if she even knew what happened, or whether Trevor kept her in the dark like the rest of us."

"Whatever she did that got her banished from Oakwood must have been pretty serious," Marc said.

"But nothing like the explosion that's liable to take place when she shows up at the dinner table tonight."

As Marc drove her home, she thought about something else that had her stumped: why had Jocelyn come back into their lives now—so soon after Kay's death?

CHAPTER ELEVEN

Lori hid in her room the rest of the afternoon: doing her nails, pondering her meager wardrobe, mustering her courage to face the evening ahead. When it came time to go downstairs, she donned a simple black chemise, added the topaz necklace Kay had given her for her twenty-fifth birthday, and slipped on a pair of three-inch heels.

As she stepped into the hall, a wave of weariness washed over her. She thought about skipping all the drama and crawling into bed with a good book. But she didn't have that luxury. Not if she was going to uncover the mystery behind Jocelyn's disappearance and the reason for her sudden reappearance. So she took a deep breath and trudged downstairs.

At first glance, it seemed as though the living room was empty. Then she caught sight of Derek by the bank of windows overlooking the woods. "Where is everyone?" she asked as she crossed the room to join him.

"Running late, I suppose." His voice sounded strained. "I guess you've heard about our dinner guest this evening."

"Marc told me." As she gazed out the window, there was a light visible through the trees in the direction of Seth's house. "I wonder where Selena's mother has been hiding all these years."

He scowled at the darkened landscape. "Who says she's been hiding?"

"Well, she certainly hasn't made any effort to

contact her daughter. At least," she hesitated, "not that I know about."

"Maybe she had a good reason for leaving."

A prickle of unease caused her shoulders to twitch. "Like what?"

He shrugged. "Ask Trevor. He's the one with all the answers."

"Walking away from her daughter seems like a heartless thing to do," she said as she studied his reflection in the glass. "Especially without putting up a fight."

He spun away from the window and stomped across the room. "You have no idea what you're talking about."

She trailed after him. "Then why don't you enlighten me."

His jaw muscle tensed. "Like I said, if you want answers, talk to Trevor."

"You know as well as I do, grown-ups never tell children the truth, especially if it puts them in a negative light. Even after their children become adults, they still cling to this out-dated need to protect them."

"Maybe it's better that way." He sank onto the sofa.

"Come on." Lori sat down beside him. "You must know something."

He gave her an angry glare. "Do I have 'family gossip' printed on my forehead?"

She refused to be intimidated by her. "Trevor is your brother."

Tension seemed to ooze from his pores. "Okay," he said. "You want to know why Jocelyn left. She left because my brother was so wrapped up in his company that he ignored her. She finally got tired of waiting for him to come to his senses, packed her bags, and headed for greener pastures."

"That can't be the whole story."

"No, it's not," he said. "But that's all I've got to say on the subject."

She came at the problem from a different angle. "I wonder why she came back now. After all these years. What changed?"

He lifted a brow. "Besides Kay's death, you mean?"

Her temple began to throb. "Besides that," she said, and was surprised by how weak her voice sounded.

Confident that he was back in control, Derek grabbed a handful of M&M's from the candy dish on the table and popped a few into his mouth. "When you think about it, her coming back here makes perfect sense."

She didn't follow his logic. "How so?"

"This is where her daughter lives."

She snorted. "If Jocelyn wanted to see her daughter so badly, why did she wait so long? She could've visited any time. Kay would've understood."

He shrugged. "Who knows? Busy earning a living probably. Or trying to please a difficult husband maybe."

That last bit startled her. But he was right. Jocelyn was too young to spend the rest of her life alone. There was probably someone special in her life. Or, maybe a string of somebodies.

"Maybe she came back to settle a score," he speculated.

She twisted around to study him. Angry blue eyes met hers. "What score would that be?"

Silence stretched between them for a long moment, then Derek said, "Everybody knows Trevor and Jocelyn had a stormy relationship. Even as kids. One time, the three of us had this club, we called ourselves 'The Survivors.' We even made a fairly decent clubhouse in an abandoned shed near the woods." He drifted away for a few seconds, caught up in memories of the past.

"And?" she asked, her curiosity sparked.

He came back to the present. "Same thing that always happened. Trevor and Jocelyn got into a fight. This time, over who was going to be club president. Since Trevor was the oldest, he thought he should be in charge. As the only straight-A student among us, Jocelyn thought she should run things. And since Trevor was bigger than both of us . . . let's just say . . . he persuaded us to see things his way. And, for awhile, everything seemed to go along fine. Until one day, after a particularly nasty disagreement, our clubhouse burned to the ground."

"Maybe someone forgot to blow out a candle," she suggested.

He shook his head. "A gasoline can was found nearby."

"Oh," she said, then added, "I didn't realize the three of you went back that far."

Derek reached for another handful of M&M's. "Seth used to be our gardener. In the summertime, he brought Jocelyn to work with him."

"Her mother didn't mind?"

"Her mother died years before." His forehead wrinkled in thought. "In childbirth, I think."

Lori felt a twinge of sympathy for Jocelyn, but didn't let that stop her from pressing home her point, "All the more reason she should've stuck around. She knows what it's like to grow up without a mother."

"Yeah, well." Avoiding eye contact, he scrambled to his feet. "If you'll excuse me, I need to make a phone call."

"Was it something I said?" she said to the empty room.

Feeling restless, she wandered over to the fireplace and studied the oil painting above the mantle. It featured a lighthouse at sunset with a flock of gulls soaring through the air.

When Trevor ambled into the room a few minutes later, he nodded toward the painting. "The artist has a small studio in Biloxi if you're interested in her work. If you like, we can . . . " His words petered out, and his eyes widened in surprise.

There could only be one reason for that startled, deer-caught-in-the-headlights, expression on his face. Lori wheeled around to find Jocelyn standing in the doorway. Tonight she had on a tight-fitting, black dress. And, in honor of the occasion, her copper-colored hair was piled atop her head, with wisps of curls framing her face. Her green eyes, so much like Selena's, danced in amusement.

Ignoring Lori, Jocelyn swept across the room to greet Trevor. An overpowering dose of some exotic perfume filled the air. "Hello, darling," she said, as if she'd just returned from an afternoon of shopping, instead of dropping back into his life some thirty years later. "The door was unlocked. I hope you don't mind that I let myself in."

The tightness about Trevor's mouth betrayed his feelings. Dispensing with the formalities, he said, "Why are you here?"

Her pencil-thin eyebrows shot up. "Is that any way to greet your wife?"

"Ex-wife," he corrected.

She flicked a manicured hand in the air. "Ex-wife then. What difference does it make?"

"I'd say the difference between night and day. Sunrise and sunset."

Tiny frown lines appeared between her eyes. "I see you haven't changed. Always worried about how things look from the outside."

Before Trevor could respond, Derek plowed into the room. "Jocelyn," he greeted their guest with genuine warmth. "You're looking as beautiful as ever."

She gave him a hug. "Hello, Derek. Still the charmer, I see."

Trevor threw his brother a look that could have melted ice. "Jocelyn was getting ready to tell us why she's here." He crossed his arms. "But since the two of you seems so chummy, maybe you already know."

"It doesn't take a genius to figure it out," Derek said. "I'm sure she heard about Kay's death and wanted to make sure her daughter's all right." He glanced at Jocelyn. "How am I doing?"

She flashed him a smile. "Excellent. As always."

Trevor's eyes darkened. "She hasn't been concerned about her daughter's well-being for the past thirty years. Why start now?"

"Because she—" Derek began.

Jocelyn laid a hand on Derek's arm, halting his words. "Derek's right. I'm here because I heard about that woman's death," she said. "I wanted to find out for myself how my baby girl's holding up."

For a moment, Lori got the distinct impression Trevor might be on the verge of throttling his ex-wife. A similar feeling stirred inside her chest. Who did Jocelyn think she was—referring to Kay as *that woman*?

Derek must have sensed Trevor's control slipping, for he deftly drew Jocelyn away. "I'm sure Selena will be down soon. Why don't we sit down and you can fill me in on what you've been up to these past few years?"

Trevor gave a snort. "Sucking money out of some unsuspecting man would be my guess." He turned away and stared into the unlit fireplace, as if he could find solace there.

Though she wasn't comfortable dispensing advice, Lori leaned over and whispered in his ear, "Don't let her get to you. She's not worth the aggravation."

He took a calming breath. "You're right," he agreed. "But you have no idea how that woman infuriates me. Waltzing in here like she owns the place. Wrapping Derek around her little finger as if he was her puppet. The woman has absolutely no conscience."

"It's your house," Lori said. "You can always ask her to leave."

His shoulders slumped. "If only it were that easy."

Of course, it was that easy. The woman was trespassing. Either she left willing, or with help from local law enforcement.

Before she could voice her opinion, an unnatural quietness settled over the room. She swung around to find Selena standing in the doorway, her face drawn and pale. Then a spark of anger ignited in those cat-green eyes, propelling her across the room to where Jocelyn was seated.

Jocelyn smiled, then held out her hand. "You must be Selena. You're even more beautiful than your grandfather said."

Ignoring the hand Jocelyn held out, Selena studied the face so much like her own. "Go home," she said coldly. "You don't belong here. I don't need you. Never have. And never will."

The smile on Jocelyn's face vanished. Her hand fell limply to her side. "I know you don't mean that." There was barely concealed pain in her voice. "I only came back to this God-forsaken town because of you. To make sure you were all right. That you could handle everything that's going on."

Selena snorted. "Where were you when I was growing up? When I actually needed a mother?"

"We have plenty of time to discuss the past." Jocelyn folded her hands in her lap. "Tonight, why don't we just enjoy being together?"

"You've got to be kidding." Selena took a step back.

"You can't expect me to spend the evening in your company. Not after you left me to fend for myself when I was just a baby."

"There's no need to get nasty." Jocelyn's voice was as cold as a frozen lake. "And for your information, I didn't leave you to fend for yourself. You had your father." She glared at Trevor. "Who, I'm sure, did a much better job of raising you than I ever could."

Emerald fire smoldered in Selena's eyes. "You didn't give him much choice, did you?"

Derek slid an arm around Selena's shoulders. "Come on, kitten. She's your mother. How about giving her a chance."

"Why?" Selena asked. "So she can abandon me again?"

As if words could crack the wall around her daughter's heart, Jocelyn began to reminisce about the past. "I'll never forget the night you were born. It was raining and the roads were slick. Your father drove as fast as he dared, but we almost didn't make it to the hospital in time." Her words grew soft, almost tender. "But we finally made it, and you were born ten minutes later. All five pounds of you. The first time I held you, you were so tiny, I was afraid your little bones might break."

Untouched by her story, Selena said, "If you cared so much, you should've stuck around and helped raise me. Or was there somewhere more important you needed to be?"

Jocelyn's gaze locked on Trevor. "Maybe you should ask your father that question. He seems to be the man with all the answers."

Selena crossed her arms. "I know his version of the story. I want to hear yours."

"Maybe you should talk about this later," Derek said, "when you don't have an audience."

Selena looked around, a sullen expression on her face. Recognizing the wisdom of his advice, she spun around and flounced across the room, taking a seat as far away from her mother as possible.

Jocelyn's attention shifted to Lori. "I don't believe we've met." She rose and swept across the room as if she were the queen of England and held out her hand.

Lagging a few steps behind, Derek made the introduction. At the mention of Lori's relationship to Kay, Jocelyn's eyes morphed into dark pools of hate. "Why are you still here? Your sister's buried. You need to go home and get on with your own life, so things can get back to normal here."

"Take it easy." Derek shot a warning look in Jocelyn's direction. "We're all family here. There's no need to get your hackles up."

Trevor straightened. "Derek's right. Lori is family." There was a hard edge to his voice. "And she's welcome to stay on as long as she likes."

"And I'm Selena's mother," Jocelyn said. "Does that mean I can stay as long as I like, too?"

"You lost the right to be part of this family a long time ago," Trevor replied.

Her lips curling in disgust, Selena bounded off the sofa and stalked toward the door. "I've had about all the family I can stand for one night."

"Hold on, kitten," Derek said, "we haven't eaten yet."

"I'll get something in town."

Seconds later, the front door slammed shut. When Derek started after her, Trevor held up a hand. "You take care of her." He nodded toward Jocelyn. "I'll talk to Selena."

"She certainly has her father's temper." Jocelyn directed her remark to Derek.

A grim look settled over his face. "And her mother's

flair for the dramatic," he added.

A few minutes later, Lou Ann stepped into the room to call everyone to the table. Her eyes made a quick sweep of the room, then, slapping her hands on her hips, said, "Least folks could do is stay around long enough to eat. I spent hours fixing all this food and there ain't hardly nobody here to enjoy it."

Derek strolled over, flung a hand around her hefty waist, and twirled her around. "Sweetheart, if it will make you feel any better, I'll eat two helpings of all that scrumptious food you've prepared."

She shoved him away and stomped back toward her kitchen. "I'm getting too old for all this nonsense."

CHAPTER TWELVE

Like condemned prisoners, Jocelyn, Derek, and Lori filed into the dining room and huddled around one end of the table. A few minutes later, Marc joined them. "Sorry I'm late." He sat down, unfolded his napkin, and glanced around. "Where is everyone?"

As they filled their plates, Derek caught him up on the situation. "Selena could've used your support," he said, with a sharp edge to his voice.

"What does she need me for?" Marc said. "When she has you wrapped around her little finger. That ought to be enough to satisfy her unending thirst for attention."

Derek wiped his mouth before answering. "You're her husband. You should have her back. Not me."

Ignoring Derek's criticism, Marc dug into his food.

Derek's jaw tightened. "Do you understand what I'm saying?"

Ignoring the question, Mark speared a piece of broccoli and popped it into his mouth.

"How did you enjoy the Smithsonian, Derek?" Jocelyn asked, hoping to defuse the situation. "Was it as wonderful as I said it would be?"

That got Marc's attention. "The Smithsonian?" His gaze shifted to Derek.

"The trip to D.C.," Derek said. When that failed to compute, he added, "The business trip Trevor insisted on sending me on."

Understanding finally dawned in Marc's eyes. "Oh right. I forgot you went to that."

"Why am I not surprised? You've been so wrapped up in that restaurant of yours, you hardly know what day of the week it is." He paused, then added, "Or have time to spend with your wife."

"I suppose that's true," Marc admitted. "The part about being busy, I mean. But now that I've got the staff pretty well trained, things should go more smoothly. I should have a little more free time."

Derek leaned back in his chair. "I hope you spend it wisely."

"How about you, Jocelyn?" Lori quickly said. "Do you get to D.C. often?"

"Not really." Jocelyn took a sip of iced tea. "I prefer more tropical climates. The Caribbean. The Bahamas. That's more my style."

"Actually," Derek said, "I invited Jocelyn to join me in D.C. I thought it was time to put an end to this feud between her and Trevor. For Selena's sake, if nothing else."

"So you two must have kept in touch over the years?" Lori directed her question at Jocelyn. "Since he knew how to get in touch with you."

Jocelyn sent a plea with her eyes to Derek for help.

"Jocelyn and I have known each other for ages," Derek said. "Just because Trevor can't get along with her, doesn't mean she and I have to be enemies."

Marc's eyes narrowed. "So you knew about this visit of hers well in advance. Probably, even encouraged it."

"I may have suggested it," Derek said. His gaze shifted to Lori. "Look, Kay was a good mother to Selena, but now that she's gone, I figured it was time for Selena to get to know her real mother."

"And I don't guess it crossed your mind to consult with Selena, or Trevor before you made these plans?" There was a dangerous edge to Marc's voice that didn't bode well for a peaceful end to their meal.

"If you're worried about Selena, don't be," Derek said. "Give her a few days to get used to the idea of having her mother around and she'll get over her little snit. You know how she is. As long as everyone's attention is focused on her, she'll milk the situation for as long as she can."

"Maybe you don't know Selena as well as you think you do." The vein along Marc's temple pulsed. "She's just lost the only mother she's ever known. Now you want her to open up, shift her loyalties to the woman who abandoned her when she was an infant. That's a lot to ask of someone."

"Believe me," Derek replied, "I know how Selena's mind works. In a lot of ways, she reminds me of myself. Once she has time to process everything, she'll be fine. Better than fine. She'll finally have the love of both her parents."

"I guess that charade at the restaurant this afternoon was—" Lori began.

"Just a head's up," Derek said.

"Look"—Jocelyn jumped into the conversation— "my visit here was just a spur of the moment decision. I was with Derek when he got the call about Kay's accident. Naturally, I was concerned about how Selena was going to take the news."

"She handled the news just fine," Marc informed her. "With no help from you, I might add."

Jocelyn's elbows shot out in a stand-your-ground stance. "Of course," she said, her voice as cold as the ice in her glass, "when I realized Lori would have to come home for the funeral, I knew I had to be here to watch my baby's back. Make sure no one tried to steal what's hers."

Was Jocelyn implying that Lori came here to steal Selena's husband?

"Don't looked so shocked," Jocelyn went on. "It's

not as if the friendship between you two was ever a secret. Several of my friends called to tell me about your engagement, then followed up when your plans fell through."

Lori felt her anger rising. "And did they mention why our plans fell through?"

Jocelyn shrugged. "Because Marc fell in love with Selena."

"More like, Selena lured Marc away because she couldn't stand for someone else to be happy," Lori said.

Jocelyn's eyes narrowed. "My daughter wouldn't need to lure any man away. She's a beautiful, talented young woman, who has been blessed with a wonderful personality."

"How would you know what kind of personality she has?" Lori said. "You never stuck around long enough to get to know her."

Jocelyn rocketed out of her chair. "It's none of your business what I did, or didn't do."

Lori scrambled to her feet. "I think Selena deserves to know the truth about why her mother abandoned her."

"She'll get the truth," Jocelyn said, "when I'm ready to tell her."

"Ladies, please," Derek broke in. "Why don't we set our differences aside and finish our meal in peace."

"I'm not the one who started this argument," Jocelyn said coolly.

"Don't blame Lori," Marc said. "She's only asking the questions we've all been wondering."

A speculative look slid across Jocelyn's face. "You're awfully quick to come to her defense."

"Yeah, well," Marc said. "I've known her a lot longer than I've known you."

"To anyone with half a brain," Jocelyn went on, "it's obvious you still have feelings for her."

It was time to set things straight. "Marc and I both grew up in this town," Lori said. "We went to school together. Worked summers together at the pizza place on Main. But as far as any romantic feelings—that's all ancient history. We're just friends now."

"Friends, huh?" Jocelyn took a step toward her. "You sure it's not more than that?"

"Positive." Lori returned her steely glare. "Now, if you'll excuse me, I have some things I need to take care of."

As she strode from the room, she heard the scrape of a chair, and Marc called out, "Wait up, Lori."

Ignoring his plea, she bolted for the stairs. He caught up with her halfway up. "Would you stop for a moment and hear me out?"

With effort, she tamped down her fury. "You have two seconds."

"Seems to me, those two are awfully anxious for you to leave. Aren't you curious why?"

"Haven't you figured it out yet?" she said. "They think there's something going on between us."

"Yeah," he said, "I got that part. But there's something else going on."

Her eyes narrowed. "You're not suggesting the two of them had something to do with Kay's death, are you?"

He shook his head. "I don't see how. Neither of them was here when Kay fell down the stairs. But there's something off about Jocelyn turning up here so soon after Kay's death."

Now that she was calmer, Lori saw the truth in what he was saying. That bulldog spirit she was famous for reared its head. No one was forcing her to leave this place until she was good and ready. "You're right," she said. "Where was all this concern for her daughter's welfare when it mattered? When she could've made a difference in her life."

The click of high heels below alerted them. Marc gave Lori a nudge, and they crept up to the second floor. From there, they had a good view of the couple below.

"Don't worry about those two," Jocelyn said. "I'll be back tomorrow and we'll decide how to handle things. In the meantime, stay calm. Otherwise, you're going to blow everything we've worked for."

Derek's reply was lost as the pair moved outside.

Lori gritted her teeth. "The nerve of that woman. Who does she think she's dealing with—a bunch of morons?"

He put a hand on her shoulder. "Forget her. We'll put our heads together and come up with a plan to beat them at their own game."

"Got any brilliant ideas about how we're going to do that?"

He shrugged. "Not at the moment. But I'm sure we'll come up with something."

"Well, it had better be soon. Or I might have to conjure up my ninja-warrior spirit and lay that woman flat on her butt."

CHAPTER THIRTEEN

The next morning, Lori was headed outside when she passed by the dining room and saw Annabel sitting at the table, sipping a cup of tea. Something about the way she was fidgeting with her cup made her pause and step to the doorway. "Is everything all right?"

"Lori, dear." Annabel made an effort to smile. "Please come join me. Everyone has been so busy these past few days; I'm afraid we haven't been the best of company."

"Don't worry about it." She slid into a chair across from Annabel. "I'm pretty good at entertaining myself."

"But you shouldn't have to entertain yourself." Annabel poured Lori a cup of lemon zinger tea. "We should be better hosts."

Lori added a cube of sugar to her tea and stirred. "It's not like I'm company."

"No, you're not company, but still . . . "

"If that's all that's bothering you . . . " She started to rise.

Annabel put a hand out to stop her. "If only it were that simple."

She sat back down. "Why don't you tell me what's wrong. Maybe I can do something to help."

After a long silence, Annabel blurted out, "It's just that woman. That contrary, good-for-nothing woman." To emphasize her point, she stamped her cane against the floor.

Startled by the unexpected outburst, Lori nearly knocked over her tea.

"Oh, I'm so sorry, dear," Annabel said. "I didn't mean to scare you. I suppose I just needed to let off a little steam. Do forgive me?"

"No harm done." She scooted forward in her seat. "Why don't you tell me exactly what the problem is, then maybe we can come up with a solution."

Annabel shook her head. "I'm afraid there's nothing you can do. But thank you for asking. It's just like that stupid woman my son was crazy enough to marry to—" Noticing Lori's reaction, she broke off. "Oh, I'm not referring to Kay, dear. She was the best thing that ever happened to Trevor. No, it's that other woman he married—Jocelyn." She spit out the name as if it were a teaspoon of some foul tasting medicine.

Lori went on high alert. "What about her?"

"She called this morning right after Trevor left for the office." Annabel hesitated, as if debating with herself whether to say more, then the words burst from her mouth, "She informed me that she would be over shortly with her things. That she'll be moving in with us until she's sure Selena's all right. She made it sound like we were nothing but a bunch of mass murderers planning to string Selena up by the neck."

Lori's blood began to boil. What right did Jocelyn have to play at being Selena's mother when she'd abandoned her all those years ago?

"Surely there must be some mistake. She can't actually believe she'd be welcome here." Her mind raced through possible scenarios for putting a stop to Jocelyn's plan. Some of them involved a little brutality. None of them worth repeating.

A frown line popped up between Annabel's eyebrows. "I'm afraid it's just the sort of stunt she would pull. As I recall, she always took great pleasure in making everyone around her miserable."

From the tone of her voice, it was clear that Annabel

was not overly fond of her former daughter-in-law. Lori wondered if there had ever been a time when they'd been close. Maybe had bonded over a shopping trip to Biloxi, or lingered over lunch at a cozy restaurant downtown.

"Oh, I do wish Trevor was here." Annabel managed a feeble smile. "Perhaps he could talk some sense into that horrible woman."

Lori reached over to cover Annabel's frail hand with her own. "I can call Trevor at the office, maybe he can—"

"I appreciate the thought, dear. But I've already tried. Mabel said he left half-an-hour ago for a business meeting in New Orleans. She doesn't expect him back until late this evening."

Not ready to give up so easily, Lori said, "I'm sure we can reach him on his cell phone."

"Mabel tried that too, but either his battery is dead, or he turned it off so he could have a little peace and quiet."

"Well, maybe Marc, or Derek could talk to her."

Annabel shook her head sadly. "I'm afraid it wouldn't do any good. Jocelyn has always been a rather strong-willed woman. Trevor was the only one who could ever reason with her." She leaned back in her seat, looking exhausted. "I guess we'll just have to make the best of things until Trevor gets home."

Hoping to take her mind off her troubles, Lori sat with her a while, engaging in pleasant conversation. Finally, Annabel shooed her away. "Do run along, dear. Do—whatever it is that you'd planned to do when you came downstairs. I think I'll go up to my room and work on the puzzle I bought last month. Can you believe it? I haven't even taken it out of the box yet."

Before heading outside, Lori insisted on helping Annabel upstairs. Once the older woman was settled with her puzzle pieces in front of her, she returned to her original plan and headed outside.

As she loped across the lawn, she caught the scent of fresh-cut grass, which, for some crazy reason, always reminded her of the smell of watermelons. The water was smooth today, not a wave in sight. About thirty yards out, a teen-age boy was hauling in a cast net.

She strolled toward the brick steps, which led to the beach. She was so occupied with scanning the water for boaters that she nearly stumbled over Selena, who was hunkered on the bottom step. "Sorry," she said, grabbing the iron railing to keep from falling over.

Selena ignored her apology. "I don't need her, you know." Her attention was focused on the glistening water.

It took a moment for Lori's mind to connect the dots. "Like it, or not—she is your mother."

"What do I need a mother for?" Green eyes, lit with anger, stared up at her. "It's not like she can hold my hand on the first day of school, or help me pick out a dress for prom."

Lori hesitated, not wanting to involve herself in Selena's problems, yet, at the same time, unable to turn away from her pain. Dropping down on the steps, she waited, giving Selena time to compose her thoughts.

"All these years I thought my mother ran off because she didn't want me. That I was nothing but a burden to her."

"Maybe she had postpartum depression," Lori offered, trying to be fair, no matter how much it galled her. "I hear it hits some women pretty hard."

Unshed tears clouded Selena's eyes. "For thirty years?"

When she was unable to supply Selena with the answers she needed, they lapsed into silence. They watched the young fisherman empty his net and move further down the beach. Occasionally, a mullet would glide through the air, then plop beneath the water's surface, leaving behind ever-widening circles.

After a while, Selena heaved herself up and scanned the woods. "He's still there. I knew he would be. He's always there. Watching me . . . waiting . . . like he expects a monster to climb out of the woods and run off with me."

Though Lori had a pretty good idea who Selena was talking about, she eased up and peered over the top of the steps. It didn't take but a moment to spot Seth behind a clump of azaleas.

"I'm sure he doesn't mean any harm," Lori said.

"Yeah, right." Selena curled her lip. "The man always has my best interest at heart."

"Cut him some slack," Lori said. "He's probably heard about your mother and wants to make sure you're all right."

"He should be more worried about her. It's not like any of us want her here." She looked thoughtful. "I wonder if he's known where she's been hiding all these years."

"Probably. I mean—she is his daughter."

"Knowing the kind of woman she is, I'm sure it was someplace expensive." She grew quiet. "I always thought Father hated me so much because I destroyed his relationship with her."

Horrified by the idea, Lori said, "Trevor doesn't . . . he would never—"

"Oh, he hides it well enough," Selena cut her off. "He says all the right things. But in my heart, I've always known. Just look at how he treats Amber. He always asks her about her day, and actually listens to her answer. Spends hours playing those silly board games with her without complaining. Even takes part in her little tea parties. He never did that for me."

"Yeah, but you're a lot older than Amber. She's just a kid. I'm sure he's learned a few things about being a father since you were that age."

Selena stiffened. "You don't have to make excuses for him. I'm used to being treated like an unwanted stepchild. Besides, I've had Grandmother." A smug look swept across her face. "And now I have Marc and Uncle Derek. I know they both love me."

Her last comment redrew the battle line, freeing Lori to walk away without guilt. "I'm sure they do." Bolting to her feet, she called out a "See you," then set off at a brisk pace down the beach.

As she strode along in the warm sand, Selena's words, "I know they love me," kept replaying through her mind. By the time she reached the point where the shoreline began its northward curve, the pain they'd brought had eased somewhat, and her aching muscles were screaming for a nice, long rest.

She collapsed on the sand and waited for her breathing to return to normal before sifting through her jumbled thoughts. So far, she was no closer to finding out who'd murdered Kay than when she'd first arrived. Though she knew Derek and Jocelyn were up to something, she couldn't tie it to Kay's death. And Selena had no motive she could pin down, other than the typical parent/child conflict that had been going on for years.

But someone had wanted Kay dead.

Trevor?

She rejected the idea as soon as it entered her mind. Trevor had loved Kay. She was the mother of his daughter. The woman carrying his precious son.

But he knew someone was terrorizing Kay, the voice inside her head chided, and did nothing to stop it.

Who did that leave? Annabel? Seth?

Annabel had always seemed genuinely fond of Kay.

Besides, she was an old lady. How could she push Kay down the stairs? And Seth was obsessed with Selena's safety and should appreciate all the effort Kay had put into raising her.

Her head began to throb. Maybe it was time to shove aside her speculations and start back. She hopped up and started walking. As she approached the house, she noticed Selena had abandoned the steps, but Seth had taken her place. Slowing her pace, she gave him ample time to slip away. Instead, he pushed to his feet and lumbered toward her.

"I wonder if I might have a word with you?" he called.

Her mind flicked to the memory of him behind a clump of azaleas spying on Selena. Her pulse quickened. "How can I help you?" she asked, trying to keep her voice steady.

"I want to talk to you about my granddaughter. I'm sure she's a mite upset about seeing her mother again. I thought, since you know her so well, you could tell me how she's handling things."

Her nervousness disappeared. "As you might expect: she's hurt, and angry that no one has told her the truth about her mother. But Selena's a fighter; she'll get through this just fine."

He grunted. "I told Trevor this would happen someday." A thick hand reached up to rub a day's growth of silver stubble. "But he wouldn't listen to me. Said there wasn't no need to upset the girl, seeing as how her mother wouldn't be coming back."

"That doesn't make any sense. Even if they were divorced, Jocelyn would still want to see her daughter. Make sure she was all right."

"You're not telling me something I don't already know. It just about broke my girl's heart—leaving her baby behind all those years ago. Especially when she found out she couldn't have no more kids."

So Jocelyn didn't leave her daughter behind willingly. "Why didn't she stick around and fight for custody of Selena? Seems like the courts generally favor the mother."

A look of defeat settled in his eyes. "Wouldn't have done no good. The Grants have been around these parts for generations. They know all the right people. My girl was the daughter of a gardener. The hired help. She never stood a chance."

Lori couldn't accept that. "But a good lawyer could've—"

"Don't need no lawyers gunking things up. All they're good for is stealing your money." He stuffed his hands in his pockets. "So you think my granddaughter's going to be all right?"

"Selena's a strong woman," she assured him. "She'll be fine."

He stood a little straighter. "I'm praying you're right; otherwise, that man will have to answer to me."

Before he could get away, she decided to do a little probing of her own. "Selena told me that you've been following her."

He wasn't embarrassed by the question. "I reckon she'd be right."

She was surprised by his candidness. "You realize you're making her uncomfortable."

"Can't be helped," he said, matter-of-factly. "Somebody's gotta' make sure she's safe."

There was that word again—safe.

"Safe from what?"

He met her gaze. "From folks that don't have her best interest at heart."

Before she could probe any deeper, he wheeled around and strode off. A feeling of confusion washed over her. Who were these *folks* Seth seemed to think his

granddaughter needed protection from?
And what did that mean for her own safety?

CHAPTER FOURTEEN

Annabel, Amber, and Lori polished off a plate of ham sandwiches for lunch. For Amber's sake, Annabel did her best to appear cheerful, but as soon as the last sandwich was eaten, she excused herself and hobbled back to her room.

Thinking it was best to keep Amber occupied outdoors until all this business about Jocelyn's moving in was settled, Lori talked her niece into posing for more pictures. "I'll even have extra copies made so you can hand them out to"—she started to say friends, then remembered Amber's claim not to have any—"to your grandmother and dad."

Amber caved in easily enough, and they set off for the gazebo. As they rounded the corner of the house, an enormous, orange-marmalade cat pounced out of the shrubbery and attacked Lori's leg. She belted out a yelp of pain that could easily be heard for miles, and had to stop herself from slugging the beast in the head with her camera bag. The only thing that saved him was the dollar signs that danced in her head at the thought of replacing any damaged equipment, and the certainty her niece would rise up to defend her beloved pet, taking out her anger on yours truly.

Before the overweight monster could inflict any more damage, Amber scooped him up. "Why are you being so mean to Watley?" A frown marred her young face. She glared at Lori as if she'd been the one doing the attacking, not the other way around. The girl nuzzled her freckled nose against the cat's neck. "Why, he's just the sweetest cat in the whole, wide world. Aren't you Watley?"

Not being a cat person, Lori was content to take her word for it. "Nice to meet you, Watley," she said, then steered both cat and girl toward the gazebo.

Once there, Amber plopped down on the nearest bench and let Watley spread out in her lap. Lori grabbed her camera and began clicking off shots of the two, while snapping out an endless stream of questions. How long have you had Watley? Who gave him to you? Does he have a favorite toy?

Experience had taught her that if she kept Amber talking, the girl would relax, become accustomed to the camera lens, and begin to look toward it as if she was looking directly into Lori's eyes. The hardest part of her job was getting a reaction. Though it only had to last a second, long enough for the click of the shutter, it took a great deal of patience.

When Lori was satisfied she'd gotten a few good shots, she clamped the lens cap back on and joined her niece on the hard-wooden bench. Signaling his displeasure, Watley cast a disdainful glance in her direction, then leaped down and trotted off.

After a few minutes, Lori said, "Penny for your thoughts."

Looking solemn, Amber shifted around to face her aunt. "Who was that woman at the house last night?" she asked, tucking a leg beneath her.

Lori gave her niece a suspicious glance. "How would you know someone was at the house last night? Your dad said you were having dinner with your grandmother. Upstairs. In her room. Well out of sight of the dining room."

Amber's cheeks turned a delicate shade of pink. "Because I sneaked downstairs while Grandma was in the bathroom."

"Good thing your dad didn't catch you."

A flicker of fear scooted across the girl's face. "You won't tell him, will you?"

Lori thought about it a moment. "As long as you promise not to do any more snooping."

Amber let out a sigh of relief. "Uh, that woman, the one who came to dinner, she kind of looked like Selena."

Lori hesitated, not sure how much she should share. "Her name is Jocelyn. Remember, you told me your parents were talking about her awhile back."

Amber frowned. "The lady that owned the ring Mommy was keeping for Daddy?"

"That's her." Lori did some quick thinking. "I don't suppose you've seen her around here before. With your dad, or uncle maybe?"

"Nope." Amber shook her head, which sent her ponytail swinging.

Lori shoved aside her disappointment. "How about we go see if Lou Ann has some chicken wings we can use for bait. Then we'll go down to the pier and catch us some crabs."

Amber grinned, then hopped off the bench. "Okay."

***

All was quiet when Lori and Amber returned to the house. After depositing their catch in the kitchen, Amber went off to her room to play with her dolls, while Lori headed to Trevor's study hoping to find something to read.

As her hand closed in on the doorknob, she heard voices inside. "I'm warning you." Jocelyn's voice rang out loud and clear. "If you make any attempt to force me to leave this house before I'm ready, I'll see to it that you regret it. And this time it will cost you a lot more than money."

Lori sucked in a breath and waited for a reply.

The answer wasn't long in coming. "It seems I have no choice but to comply. For the moment, anyway. But let's get one thing clear"—a note of restrained anger lent a chill to his voice—"I'll only be pushed so far. After that, you take your chances."

Footsteps thudded toward the door, forcing Lori to scurry down the hallway and duck into the living room. She barely had time to plop down on the couch and grab a magazine from the coffee table before Trevor breezed into room. "I had no idea you were interested in sport fishing," he said, dropping down beside her.

As her face flushed with heat, she tossed the magazine aside. "You know me, I'm always interested in learning new things."

"Is that so?" He called her bluff. "There's a tournament coming up in June. Maybe I should sign us up. I have to warn you though—you'll be responsible for putting your own bait on the hook."

She wrinkled her nose. "I'll probably be too busy this summer to take another vacation."

"Hmmm." He smiled knowingly. "That's what I figured."

A few minutes later, Jocelyn poked her head through the doorway. "Derek said we'd be dining outside tonight. Are you ready to head out that way?"

Vertical creases marred Trevor's forehead. "I thought you had an appointment in town tonight."

She shrugged. "Nothing I couldn't reschedule."

"Just our luck." He stood up and motioned Lori to precede him. Trailing behind them, Jocelyn muttered something about the lousy manners of men these days.

To an outsider, the assembled group probably looked like the typical American family gathered around the table to share a meal and exchange pleasantries. But to those present, the tension was as thick as mud. Not even the sound of Bach drifting from the house could soothe their troubled souls.

Even Lou Ann seemed to sense the mounting tension. She bustled outside carrying a platter of fried chicken, dumped it on the table, then hurried inside for the trappings. With the extra pair of hands Marc lent, they were soon ready to eat.

Even though the food was tasty, no one seemed to have much of an appetite. Throughout the meal, Jocelyn kept up a stream of chatter, as if this was just an ordinary day, and she had always been part of the family.

As soon as desert was served—huge slices of apple pie, topped with vanilla ice cream—Selena pushed back her plate, mumbled something about needing to fill a special order, and hurried off to her workshop. Soon after, Amber ran inside to play with the new doll Trevor had brought back from his trip to New Orleans, while the rest of the family remained trapped at the table, sharing a pot of coffee.

Annabel waited until Derek and Jocelyn wandered off, then got down to business. "I want to know why that horrible woman is still here?" There was a glint of anger in those faded blue eyes.

Trevor's gaze flicked toward Lori and Marc. "Maybe we should discuss this later."

"We'll talk about it now, young man," Annabel said. "I've seen quite enough of that woman. I didn't like her when you married her; I like her even less now."

Trevor grabbed a teaspoon and stirred the remnants of his coffee. "She's here because of Selena." He refused to meet his mother's gaze. "With all that's happened, Selena needs her mother to help her deal with her . . . issues."

"Poppycock." Annabel stamped her cane against the brick floor. "I'm old, not senile. I want to know the real reason why you haven't sent that woman packing. The

Trevor I raised would have thrown the little hussy out of here the minute she walked through the door."

"Believe me, I did my best to send her packing." His voice sounded strained. "But she took great pleasure in assuring me that, unless we want certain facts leaked to the press, we'd better let her stay until she's ready to leave."

While Trevor explained the situation, Lori kept her eyes fixed on Annabel. The older woman's face drained of color, and her shoulders sagged. The cane clutched in her hand tumbled to the pavement.

"Don't upset yourself, Mother." Trevor retrieved his mother's cane and hooked it on the arm of her chair. "Jocelyn is my problem, not yours. Let me deal with her."

"You shouldn't have to deal with her. She has no business tearing our family apart again."

"Well, she's back, and it doesn't look like she's going away anytime soon. At least, not without a fight. Which I'm not sure we can win this time."

"The nerve of that woman. Showing up here, making threats. After all you've done for her."

He shrugged. "Maybe she really wants to get to know her daughter better. But she has no idea how stubborn Selena can be. Once she figures out how much work it involves, I'm sure she'll get over this motherhood-fantasy and crawl back into the sewer she climbed out of."

Annabel rallied. "It can't happen soon enough. That woman nearly destroyed this family once. I will not stand by and allow her to do it again."

"I vote for kicking her to the curb," Marc quickly voiced his opinion. "From what I've heard, the woman's nothing but trouble. Letting her stay might push Selena into another meltdown."

Trevor studied his son-in-law. "And if we don't let

her stay, things might get a whole lot worse for all of us."

A shiver snaked up Lori's spine. How much worse could it get? Though everyone pretended Kay's death had been an accident, she knew her sister had been murdered. A woman no one seemed to trust had forced her way into their mist. Now Selena, known for her reckless behavior, might be headed for a meltdown.

Pasting on a weak smile, Annabel stood up. "It's been a rather tiring day. If you'll excuse me, I think I'll go upstairs now and rest. Perhaps if we're lucky that woman will be gone by morning."

When Marc insisted on escorting Annabel to her room, Lori tagged along. Once Annabel was settled in a chair by the window, she shooed them away, saying she wanted to work on her puzzle a few minutes before she went to bed.

As they entered the living room, Marc asked, 'Do you have any idea what this big secret is that Trevor was talking about?"

"I've been away from here for the past seven years." She plopped down on the sofa. "You'd be more likely to know what he's talking about than I would."

"The first I heard about any secret was the morning Selena and her grandmother got into it." He strolled to the window and peered out. "I wonder if it's the reason Derek left town all those years ago."

"Could be." She slipped off her shoes and tucked one leg under her. "Derek and Trevor don't seem to get along all that well. Imagine what they must've been like as testosterone-fueled adolescents."

Marc drifted away from the window and slid into the chair beside her. "Lots of brothers are like that. How does that old saying go? 'Just because you're born into a family, doesn't mean you have to like them.'? Sometimes personalities just clash."

"I wonder if Selena knows what happened between the brothers?"

"Hard to say." He leaned over and grabbed a handful of M&M's from the bowl on the table. "She keeps a lot of stuff to herself. I never realized she liked to draw until a couple of years ago when I found some of her old sketch pads tucked away in the attic."

"I forgot she used to carry around a sketch pad in her book bag," she said. "I have no idea if her drawings were any good. Whenever I tried to get a look, she'd shove it back in her bag and tell me to quit being a pest."

"Sometimes, I wonder if I even know her," he confessed. "If it's even possible to know what's going on in that mind of hers. She has this whole side that she keeps hidden from everyone. Including me."

She didn't want to get sucked into a conversation about the complexities of Selena's personality, so she told him about the conversation she had overheard between Trevor and Jocelyn in the study.

"Sounds as if our knight definitely has a few chinks in his armor," he said, stuffing another handful of M&M's into his mouth.

She felt her shoulders deflate. "Maybe."

"From what you've told me—there's no maybe about it."

"But Trevor has always been so solid . . . so . . . dependable."

"Because you were always looking at him through rose-tinted glasses." He scooted forward in his chair. "He's the man who married your sister, the man who took over the father role in your life. It's no wonder you're having trouble accepting the idea that he may have a few flaws. You don't want him to fall off that pedestal you've put him on."

She bounded off the sofa. "We don't have any proof

that Trevor has some dark secret. Only Jocelyn's accusation. And what we know about her could fit on a thimble. She could be an ax murderer, for all we know."

He grinned. "Not likely."

"Okay," she said, growing agitated, "maybe not an ax murderer, but certainly a troublemaker."

"That, I'll buy."

"She has no right to come in here and try to take Kay's place. Kay was a good mother to Selena. And she didn't run off the moment things got tough."

"You'll get no argument from me." There was a long pause, then he added, "What does concern me is this threat to ruin Trevor's reputation if he tries to force her to leave before she's ready." He quirked up an eyebrow. "As Ricky Ricardo would say, 'He has a lot of 'splainin to do.' "

"Okay." She threw up her hands in surrender. "Maybe you're right. Trevor may have a few flaws. But I have a hard time believing he could do anything dishonorable."

"Those rose-tinted glasses again," he reminded her.

She knew there was some truth in what he said. She barely remembered her own father. She wanted to believe—needed to believe—Trevor wasn't capable of deceit on such a grand scale.

"What was all that about Selena having a meltdown?" she asked. "I don't remember anything like that ever happening."

"We figured the fewer people who knew, the better." He seemed to have a hard time getting the words out. "After our son . . . Timmy . . . passed away, she checked out there for awhile. I had to admit her to a psychiatric hospital."

"Oh." She was at a loss for words. "I had no idea. She's always been so strong. I never realized . . . "

He sighed. "I'm only telling you now, because I thought it might help you understand how delicate her mental state is."

Lori scrolled through her mind searching for times when she might have pressed Selena too hard, pushed her into another breakdown. "She hasn't had any more episodes, right?"

"No," he was quick to reassure her. "I guess I'm just being cautious. But with all that's been going on lately, I worry it could happen again."

"Kay's death. Her mother suddenly appearing. I can see how that might elevate her stress level."

"So you'll take it easy on her," he said. "Drop all this murder nonsense?"

She was filled with warring emotions. On one hand, she didn't want to be responsible for driving Selena into the loony bin. On the other hand, whoever killed Kay deserved to be punished.

"I'll think about it," she promised.

CHAPTER FIFTEEN

Saturday morning, Lori stayed in bed until ten-thirty. She blamed her laziness on the restless night she'd had. Since Lou Ann had the weekend off, Lori snagged an apple from the fruit bowl in the kitchen and wandered outside. She remembered Marc telling her that Selena had converted the old tool shed into a workshop for her ceramics. Curious to get a look inside, she headed that way.

Peering through the front window, she saw Selena hunched over the counter working on a clay figurine. This morning she was dressed simply: jeans and soft green T-shirt, with a baggy blue apron tied about her waist.

When Selena caught sight of her, she said, "Don't just stand there gawking. Come inside. Maybe you'll learn something."

As she stepped inside, Selena motioned to the barstool next to the counter. "Have a seat," she said. A fiery lock of hair fell across one eye. She batted it away with the back of her hand and kept working.

Lori crawled onto the stool and studied the piece Selena was working on. "Is this something new?" She gestured toward the work-in-progress, trying to recall if she'd seen anything like it in Selena's Corner.

Selena nodded. And seemed pleased that she'd noticed. "I needed to freshen up my inventory. I thought I'd give this a try and see how it goes."

She watched in fascination as Selena reached for a piece of cotton netting that had been soaking in slip.

After blotting out the excess, she began fastening the material to the form she was working on, making folds about the waist, which she then pressed into position with a pointed modeling tool. "The cotton will burn out in the kiln leaving its pattern behind in the dress," Selena explained.

After watching her work for awhile, Lori slid off the stool and began to explore the room. Sturdy bookshelves covered three walls, filled with an assortment of both finished and unfinished pieces, along with several stacks of molds. A large kiln occupied the back left corner, while a potter's wheel took up most of the area under the front window.

Aware of her interest, Selena said, "It's a double-cone drive wheel. Marc gave it to me for Christmas."

As she moved over to take a closer look, there was a sharp rap on the door. A moment later, the door popped open and Jocelyn stepped inside. "I thought you might—" Jocelyn caught sight of Lori and frowned. "Sorry." She turned to go. "I didn't realize you had company."

"That's okay," Lori called out. "I was just leaving."

Selena quickly moved to block her path. "You can't go yet. I haven't had a chance to show you around."

There was a pleading look in Selena's eyes that she couldn't ignore. Nodding consent, she strolled over to examine a finished piece shaped like a Magnolia blossom, giving mother and daughter some semblance of privacy.

Jocelyn didn't seem all that pleased by the arrangement, but there was little she could do about it, short of tossing Lori out on her tush. So she did the next best thing—simply ignored her. "Nice work," she said, motioning toward the figurine in the center of the workbench.

Selena shrugged. "It'll do."

Trying to stay out of the line of fire, Lori studied the pieces displayed on the shelves along the back wall, picking up a piece, here and there.

"I've been by your shop." Jocelyn took another stab at winning her daughter's favor. "It's very impressive. I particularly like—"

"What do you want?" Selena laid down her modeling tool.

Jocelyn seemed to recoil at the harshness in Selena's voice. "I don't want anything. I just thought we could hang out together. You know, do the mother/daughter bonding thing."

"I'm not interested in—"

"Please." Jocelyn cut her off. "I just want a chance to get to know you. I've missed so much of your life already. I have no idea what kind of student you were. Or what kind of foods you like. Or even if you had any training for this." She gestured toward the figure Selena was working on.

Selena's face hardened. "It's a little late to play the caring mom, don't you think?"

Jocelyn took a deep breath. "I know it must seem like I didn't care about you, but that's not true. I thought about you every single day. It's just that . . . circumstances . . . prevented me from being there for you."

"It doesn't matter," Selena said. "I had Father, and Kay. I got by just fine. So you can ditch the martyr act."

"Kay." Jocelyn made a dismissive gesture. "She was barely a kid herself when your father married her. What did she know about being a mother?"

Selena dug her nails into the counter. "Let me guess. Now comes the part about how leaving me behind almost killed you. How you were so depressed that you had to self-medicate with pills and alcohol."

"Baby, I don't blame you for being angry." Her eyes

pleaded for forgiveness. "In your place, I'd probably be angry, too. But you have no idea what my life was like then. What Trevor was—is—capable of."

"I'm not your baby," Selena snapped. "And, at least, he had the decency to stick around, make sure there was food on the table and clothes on my back. That's more than you ever did."

Realizing this might be her only opportunity to hear Jocelyn's side of the story, Lori said, "Maybe you should give her a chance to tell her side of the story." At Selena's fierce glare, she added, "Or not."

Jocelyn tossed Lori a grateful smile, then turned back to Selena. "If you'd just listen to what I have to say, not believe all that rubbish your dad's been feeding you, I know you'll be able to forgive me."

Selena offered no objection, so Jocelyn took a deep breath and began, "I was just a young girl when your dad and I married—barely nineteen. He was putting in long hours at work and barely knew I existed. Then, before I even had time to get used to being a wife, I found myself pregnant with you." She leaned against the workbench. "You have no idea how lonely I was."

Selena didn't cut her any slack. "And my life has been all sunshine and rainbows."

Jocelyn flinched. "I'm sorry you got caught in the middle of our problems. But like I said, I was young and inexperienced." She retreated to the large window near the front door. "I realize now, I could've handled things better. No matter what the situation was like between your father and me, I should have stuck around and fought for custody of you. But at the time, it seemed like the right thing to do."

"But Selena was your own flesh and blood," Lori said. "How could you leave her behind, especially if Trevor was too busy with work to care for her? If it hadn't been for Annabel and Kay, no telling what would've happened to her."

"Trevor didn't need me to take care of his daughter." Jocelyn looked ready to throttle someone. "Like you said, he had his precious mother to take care of her. And his sainted wife." She glared at Lori. "And I don't see how any of this is your business. You're not even part of our family."

Selena stood up. "But it is my business."

"Of course it is, baby," Jocelyn hurried to make amends. "But maybe we should take our time, get to know each other better, before we delve into all this past history."

There was controlled fury in Selena's response. "I don't see how we can have a relationship unless we delve into your reason for leaving me."

Jocelyn hugged herself. "It's complicated."

"In case you haven't noticed, I'm not a child anymore," Selena said. "I get that you were unhappy in your marriage. We've all been there. But that doesn't explain why you abandoned me."

"Maybe she has a valid reason for leaving," Lori said, trying to be fair.

"You keep out of this," Selena said. Sparks of anger zinged toward Lori. "I don't know why you butted into my business in the first place. If my father hadn't married your sister . . . "

She didn't need to finish the thought. Lori knew where she was headed. If her sister hadn't married Selena's father, then Selena's parents might have patched things up. It was the delusion common to all children of divorce.

"You're right. I should've stayed. If I had to do it over,"—Jocelyn smiled sadly—"I would do things differently."

Selena snorted. "I'm sure you would."

Ignoring her daughter's comment, Jocelyn went on

with her story. "The only bright spot in my life back then was your Uncle Derek. Unlike your dad, he always had time for me. We spent a lot of time walking along the beach together, talking about everything that was going on in our lives. Then in the evenings, we'd hunker down and play cards. I honestly don't think I would've survived without him."

For some reason, the mention of Derek's name sent a new wave of anger surging through Selena's veins. She snatched up the figurine she'd been working on and sent it sailing across the room. Luckily, Jocelyn ducked before the piece slammed into her head. The window, however, did not fare as well. Shards of glass flew everywhere.

When Jocelyn straightened up, a trickle of blood oozed down her arm. "What on earth is the matter with you? I could've been seriously injured by that—thing." She swept a hand in the air for emphasis.

Selena snatched up a clay pot. "Get out." Her gaze shifted from Jocelyn to Lori. "Both of you."

Without further prompting, the two barreled out the door like a pair of racehorses. And didn't slow down until they reached the house, where they parted ways.

CHAPTER SIXTEEN

By early afternoon, the warm, sunny weather had vanished. Black clouds rolled in, punctuated by angry gusts of wind. Pounding rain soon followed. Lori wandered from room to room, finally settling in the living room with Trevor, Annabel, and Amber. Every few minutes, she would stroll over to the window to check on the storm's progress.

"What happened to all those family albums you used to have?" she asked Annabel on one of her return trips.

Annabel had to think about it for a minute. "Seems like Selena hauled them up to the attic when Kay was having the floors redone last year."

It had been a long time since Lori had poked around in the attic. Who knew what interesting items might be tucked away up there. She might even come across something that could shed some light on this *family secret* everyone was so reluctant to talk about. "Would you mind if I go up and look for them?"

"Of course not, dear," Annabel said. "If I'm not mistaken, Selena put them in an old army trunk she found up there. Along the back wall, I think."

Amber sat her doll aside. "I want to go, too."

Trevor shook his head. "No way, young lady. I don't want you up there. The place is full of dusty, old junk. Most of it should've been thrown away years ago."

When no amount of pleading could persuade him to change his mind, Lori grabbed a flashlight from the kitchen and headed upstairs.

The key to the attic was hanging on a hook in the

hallway. After unlocking the door, she put the key back where she'd found it. The door creaked as it swung open. She fumbled around for the light switch, which was somewhere on the right. She flipped it on, then made her way up the stairs.

Here, illumination came from a single row of bare bulbs. Surveying the array of castoffs, she realized the enormity of her task. There were enough boxes to fill a warehouse, along with a hodgepodge of furniture, and a general mishmash of other items. In other words: the place was full of dusty, old junk just like Trevor had said it would be.

Good thing Annabel had given her a general location to start her search; otherwise, she might be here all day. Thankfully, the floors were made of good, solid pine, so there was no danger of falling through. The real problem was—the jumble of items between here and the back wall.

She began her journey by easing around a battered oak dresser with several missing knobs. By pure luck, she discovered a semi-trail through the chaos. Problem was the further along the trail she moved, the narrower it grew.

She was about halfway to her goal when her blouse got snagged on an antique baby carriage. As she stopped to untangle it, the skin on the back of her neck started to tingle. She glanced around, but saw nothing to justify her unease. Still, the feeling wouldn't go away.

Her survival instinct screamed for her to hit the stairs and not look back. But her uncover-the-truth-at-all-costs gene urged her to plow ahead. Feeling foolish, she shook off her concerns and renewed her effort to reach the back wall.

Overhead, rain hammered against the roof drowning out all sounds from below, making her feel even more isolated. She paused here and there to examine the markings on the boxes she encountered: baby items, miscellaneous kitchenware, extra linens, but found no label marked—Grant family secrets.

Finally, she located the battered metal chest where the albums were stored. She bent down and flipped open the lid. A huge stack of photo albums was inside, along with half a dozen shoeboxes containing loose pictures. There was no way she could cart everything downstairs. She'd have to sort through the items here and take only the most interesting with her.

After a brief search, she found an Early American rocker with a broken spindle and dragged it over to sit on. She stowed her flashlight on the floor beside her, grabbed a couple of albums, and began to flip through the pages. The first one seemed to be the history of Selena's life, from birth to around school age. She noticed Jocelyn wasn't in any of the pictures. Setting aside the album, she reached for the next one.

A soft, rustling noise near the door caught her attention. Maybe Trevor had relented and was bringing Amber to join her. Leaning over, she peered around a stack of boxes. "Is someone there?"

There was no answer.

Chalking it up to an overactive imagination, she returned to her perusal of Selena's life through pictures. The next album picked up where the other left off, documenting Selena's elementary school days. Lots of pictures of Selena, Trevor, and Annabel, but none of Jocelyn. Another thing that struck her as a bit odd, there were no pictures of Derek, either.

As she opened the next album, a crash of thunder rattled the house. Startled, she leaped to her feet, sending the album in her lap crashing to the floor. Time to move the history lesson downstairs. She grabbed an armful of albums and fled toward the door.

She was halfway there when the attic was plunged into darkness. Had lightning struck a transformer? Were the lights out all over the house? Or was the blackout confined to the attic?

A floorboard creaked up ahead. She froze in place and listened, but all was quiet. Sighing with relief, she tucked the albums under one arm and felt her way along the narrow passage toward the door.

Another sound came. Closer this time. Possibly the scrape of furniture against the floor.

She stopped moving. Held her breath. And listened.

Was someone deliberately trying to frighten her?

"Selena is that you?" she called out.

Silence.

"Joke's over," she said firmly, wishing she'd thought to grab the flashlight off the floor before racing for the door. "Time to turn the lights back on before someone gets hurt," she added when there was no response.

She got the distinct impression someone was nearby, waiting for her response. Her mind raced through options. She could scream at the top of her lungs and hope someone heard, which wasn't likely with the rain hammering the roof. Or, she could throw something toward the spot where the sound came from, which was probably too risky, considering it might block her access to the door. Her final option was to slither into a hiding spot and hope the person who had turned out the lights would go away. Which might actually work, if she didn't trip over something and break her neck in the process.

A raspy whisper came from somewhere on her left. "This is your last warning. Go home, or you'll be next."

A beam of light slammed into her face. Acting on instinct, she threw up a hand to shield her eyes, just as a heavy object whizzed past her shoulder.

Then the light blinked out.

A heavy dose of adrenaline poured into her veins. She tossed the albums aside and charged back down the trail, stumbling into objects, knocking things over, and banging her hip on something hard.

After what seemed like endless minutes, she located the trunk, dropped to her knees, and groped around, searching for her own flashlight.

Couldn't find it. Tried not to panic. Tried to get control of her breathing.

Suddenly, the other light flicked back on, zeroed in on her location. She abandoned her search for the flashlight and crouched behind a pile of discards. Her knee came into contact with a hard metal cylinder. Stifling a yelp, she picked it up. Her fingers raced up and down, searching for the switch.

Before she could locate it, something heavy slammed into her body. She grunted, then fell, face first, into the floor. On the way down, her shoulder hit something hard, sending a tsunami of pain through her body. She struggled to roll over, but couldn't free herself from the massive object, which pinned her to the floor.

That's when the screaming began.

Then something heavy came down on her skull, and the screaming abruptly stopped.

CHAPTER SEVENTEEN

Lori came to in her own bed. Annabel was perched in a chair beside her, her forehead wrinkled in worry. She tried to sit up, assure Annabel she was all right, but a blinding pain tore through her head, forcing her back down.

"There, there, dear, don't even think about getting out of this bed. Trevor went next door to get our neighbor. He's a doctor. I'm sure he'll be happy to come over and take a look at you. You just lie there and rest until he gets here."

Despite the pain, Lori inched back up. She wanted—needed—to tell someone what had happened in the attic. "Somebody tried to . . . " she began. Her throat felt like raw meat. She tried again. "Someone—" Before she could get the words out, Trevor bustled through the doorway.

When he realized she was awake, he darted across the room and began to bombard her with questions. Seconds ago, she was ready to share her story. Now, some instinct made her hold back. "I'm okay," her voice sounded gravelly. "I just tripped over something when the lights went out and banged my head."

The lie sounded lame, even to her ears. Before Trevor was able to badger her with more questions, a short, bald man flew into the room carrying a black satchel and shooed everyone out of the room.

After his examination, Doc Sanders suggested a stay in the hospital overnight for observation. Lori immediately nixed the idea. "I figured that might be your answer." Reaching into his satchel, he took out a bottle of pills and shook out a couple of tablets. "Here, take these. Then it's bed rest for you, young lady. For the next couple of days, at least. And while you're lying there, you might take advantage of Lou Ann's cooking. You could stand to put on a few pounds."

Why was everyone always trying to fatten her up?

Before the doctor left, he gave Annabel a list of things to be on the alert for: blurred vision, vomiting, slurred speed, or loss of coordination. Rising to the occasion, she shooed Trevor out of the room, then stood guard over her patient the rest of the evening.

Grateful for the reprieve, Lori nestled under the covers. Despite her best efforts, scenes from the attic began to replay through her mind. She searched for clues that would narrow down her list of suspects—something distinctive about the voice she'd heard, or something familiar about the way her assailant moved. But she couldn't come up with anything. It had been too dark, and everything had happened so fast.

Eventually, she drifted to sleep.

***

Annabel had her way, and Lori was confined to bed for the next two days. On the third day, she was allowed to get up, but with the caution not to overdo.

The first opportunity she got, Lori headed for the attic. Though it had been two days, she hoped to find a clue that would shed some light on her assailant's identity. What she hadn't counted on was the blind panic that shot through her body the moment she unlocked the door.

What if someone was lurking nearby . . . watching . . . . waiting . . . ready to attack her again?

A shiver worked its way up her spine. It took every ounce of courage she could muster to step inside, flip on the light switch, and march upstairs. The place appeared to be empty, but that could be an illusion. On shaky limbs, she began to weave her way through the mountain of castoffs toward the back wall.

The photo albums she'd been looking through were no longer lying on the floor, but were neatly stacked inside the trunk. She surveyed the area, looking for anything out of place.

Nothing stood out.

She turned her attention to finding the object her assailant—someone she probably thought of as family—had used to clunk her over the head. It had to be small enough to lift easily, yet hefty enough to render a person unconscious. She found all sorts of objects fitting that description, but none with smears of blood, or strands of hair stuck to their surface.

Next, she searched the area where she thought the voice had come from and discovered a spot behind an old bookcase where the dust had been disturbed. Dropping down on one knee, she hunted for a clear footprint, a scrap of fabric, anything that might indicate who had attacked her.

But, again, she found nothing.

She was ready to give up when she spotted a gold bracelet caught on the seat of a frayed, cane rocker. It was a beautiful piece, two slender braids wound together with some kind of leaf-patterned filigree across the middle. She was no expert, but it appeared to be real gold.

The thump of footsteps on the stairs sent her body into a state of high alert. She looked around for something to defend herself with. Found a broken lamp on a nearby table. She snatched it up, ready to do battle with the person who came through the doorway.

"Don't panic," Selena called as she plowed into the room. "It's just me."

Some of the tension drained from Lori's body. She returned the lamp to the table. "What are you doing here? I just about crushed your skull."

"You need to chill out. I'm not the enemy here."

Heat suffused Lori's face. "Sorry. But after what happened the other day, I guess I'm a little jumpy."

Selena seemed to accept her apology. "You've been up here a really long time. I thought I'd better check on you, make sure you hadn't run into more trouble."

"How did you know I was up here?" Lori heard the challenge in her voice, but didn't back down.

"Who else would be crazy enough to be snooping around up here?"

Before Lori could answer, another voice boomed from below. "Who's up there?" Footsteps pounded up the stairs. A moment later, Trevor appeared. His hair was a tousled mess. His glance slid past his daughter and settled on Lori. "I thought you were supposed to be taking it easy."

Irritated, Lori snapped back, "I'd appreciate it if everyone would quit treating me like an invalid. As you can see, I'm perfectly fine."

Trevor closed his eyes and pressed his fingertips against his temples. "Maybe we should head downstairs and have something cold to drink," he suggested.

As he turned to go, Lori blurted out, "I found something."

He halted in his tracks and turned slowly around. Lori held up the bracelet. Trevor's gaze shifted from the bracelet to Selena. "I don't think—" he began.

"That's mine. Father gave it to me for my birthday last year." She snatched the bracelet from Lori's hand. "I must've lost it the other day in all the excitement."

Before or after you slammed something down on my head? Lori wanted to ask, but settled for, "Don't you want to know where I found it?"

"Not particularly." She scurried toward the stairs. "It's back now. That's all that matters."

Trevor stepped aside to let her pass. Noting the concern on Lori's face, he said, "She probably lost it when she was helping us get you back to your room." He hesitated, then added, "I don't know if anyone told you, but Selena was the one who found you and called for help."

No one had told her, and it had never occurred to her to ask. Which underscored how muddled her thinking had become.

Feeling her energy sag, she mumbled something about feeling tired and trudged back to her room. For nearly an hour, she managed to take it easy. She sat by the window and flipped through the stack of magazines Annabel had left by her bedside. She climbed into bed and tried to sleep. Finally, she gave up on the whole resting idea, grabbed her camera case off the dresser, and headed outside to get some fresh air.

At first, she wandered around taking shots of the various plants on the grounds. When she grew bored with that, she ventured into the woods. It wasn't long before she stumbled upon the perfect spot for taking photos. A spot where someone, most likely Seth, had spread birdseed. The whole area crawled with wildlife. Of course, the moment Lori stepped into the clearing, the menagerie scattered.

Confident her newfound friends would return, she unfolded her tripod beside a clump of bushes and attached her camera. She took a reading with her light meter, adjusted the f-stop, and then settled down in a nest of leaves, the cable release in hand, to wait.

How rich and green the world seemed from down here. Above her head, soft puffs of wind stirred the leaves, causing them to dance in the sunlight. The only sounds to be heard were the twitter and whir of birds, and the occasional hum of a plane as it soared through the sky.

After she'd sat there awhile, a plump, gray squirrel eased into the clearing. She waited . . . waited . . . until he reached for a sunflower seed, then pressed the release button. Sensing danger, the squirrel scampered back to the safety of a nearby oak.

Before the afternoon was over, she took several more shots of her adventurous squirrel friend, plus numerous shots of blue jays, cardinals, and various other feathered creatures. By the time she packed up her equipment, it was growing late. Once again, work had come to her rescue, calming her fears, providing a focus for her thoughts when life became too overwhelming.

As she slung her camera case over her shoulder, a twig snapped behind her. Panic zinged through her body. She wheeled around and saw Marc standing along the edge of the clearing. "Oh, it's you." Her voice sounded uncharacteristically high and squeaky.

"Of course, it's me. Who were you expecting—the Pope?"

A grin tugged up the corners of her mouth. "More like the devil in disguise."

"I thought you were supposed to be taking it easy."

"What could be easier than this?" She lifted a hand to the sky. "A peaceful spot in the woods with only the animals for company."

Marc's face grew serious. "What concerns me is the alone part. After what happened in the attic, seems like you'd have the good sense not to run off on your own."

"I can't stay cooped up in that house forever. And"—she held up a hand—"as you can see, I'm fine."

"This time," he said. "But what about the next time someone comes after you? You might not be so lucky."

"I can't live my life in fear."

Worry lines marred his face. "But you could be more cautious. Stay with the group. Not go running off on your own."

Her cheeks burned with embarrassment. "I guess I should've told someone where I was going," she conceded, "so no one would worry."

"You bet you should have." He paused, then went on to add, "Look, we've enjoyed your company, but maybe it's time to pack up your things and head home."

She felt her temper start to rise. "I'll go home when I finish what I came to do." She lifted her head, then stalked off down the trail.

"Hey, don't get mad." He plowed after her and snagged her arm, "I'm only trying to look out for you."

"I can look out for myself. If you feel the need to take care of someone, you might want to start with Selena. After all, she is your wife."

When she tried to pull away, he tightened his grip. "We both know Selena wasn't my first choice. The woman I'd planned to spend the rest of my life with ran off and left me." His gray eyes were clouded with pain. "What I never understood is: why she would do that to me—to us?"

Lori's temper edged a notch higher. "You know perfectly well why I left. When Selena came up pregnant—"

"Forget about Selena. If you really loved me, you wouldn't have run off like that."

Her shoulders slumped. "Okay." She decided to be honest. "Maybe Selena was only part of the problem. Maybe the real reason I left was because . . . because I was afraid."

Startled, he let go of her arm. "Afraid of what?"

How could she make him understand her feelings when she didn't understand them herself? "That what we had wouldn't last. That you'd be like my father. That you'd wake up one morning, decide you'd made a mistake, and take off."

He shook his head in disbelief. "I'm not that kind of

man."

"You could've fooled me," she said. "How long did it take you to crawl into bed with Selena after I left?"

He winced.

"Two months, if I remember correctly." She glared at him. "I thought you had more sense than to fall for her helpless female act."

He shoved back a clump of hair. "Yeah, well. At the time, I didn't realize she only wanted me to make you jealous. She did a pretty good job of convincing me we were soul mates, destined to spend our lives together."

She shook her head in disgust. "I just bet she did."

"By the time I came to my senses, it was too late. Believe me, when you first left, I did everything I could to find you. I pestered Kay for weeks trying to find out where you'd gone, but she wouldn't tell me anything."

"Because she didn't know."

"Eventually, I figured that out."

Crossing her arms, she stared off into the distance. "I didn't tell her because I didn't want to involve her in our problems."

"You realize, disappearing like that—without a word to anybody—nearly drove Kay out of her mind. She was convinced you didn't leave town under your own power. Trevor had to talk her out of filing a missing person's report. We both called everyone we could think of, but no one had heard from you."

"Because I didn't want to be found. I needed time to clear my head. And I couldn't do that here." There was a long silence, then she asked tentatively, as if afraid of hearing his answer, "Why didn't you wait for me?"

He sighed. "Because Selena convinced me that you didn't want me. That you didn't love me enough to stay and try to work things out. And she was always there, telling me how wonderful I was, offering me a shoulder to lean on. So I settled. I'm not proud of it, but that's what I did."

"Did Selena realize how you felt? About me, I mean?"

"She knew. But then she got pregnant"—he looked away—"I couldn't abandon her. Leave her with a baby to raise on her own."

She heard the pain in his voice. Knew part of it was caused by her desertion; the other part, from a child's life that ended before it really began.

"I never told you how sorry I was about Timmy."

His jaw tightened. "It was a long time ago." He seemed to go somewhere within himself for a moment. Then, he forced himself back into the here-and-now. "I'm sure you know, Selena and I haven't had an ideal marriage. But you have to give her credit, she's stuck by me, even though she's always known my heart belongs to—"

Lori held up a hand. "It's too late for regrets."

"I know." There was a deep sadness in his voice. "I just wish things had turned out differently, that's all."

CHAPTER SEVENTEEN

The next morning, Lori came downstairs to find Selena and Jocelyn huddled around the dining room table. After pouring herself a much-needed cup of coffee, she slid into the seat across from Jocelyn.

"I was beginning to think you'd never get up." Selena glanced at her watch. "I've been waiting on you for at least twenty minutes." She laced her fingers together and glared at Lori.

Lori raked through her memory, trying to figure out what she'd done to upset Selena, and came up empty.

"I can't believe you don't remember."

As memory returned—the postponed lunch date due to her misfortune in the attic—Lori's cheeks grew warm. "Isn't it a little early for lunch? I haven't even had my first cup of coffee yet."

"Yes, well. Our plans have changed. We have to leave earlier than I told you."

Lori's stomach growled. "How much earlier?"

"As soon as you can change out of those shorts and put on something suitable."

"I thought we were going shopping," Jocelyn protested.

"We'll have to do that some other time," Selena said. "Lori and I have other plans for today."

"Then I'll grab my things and come with you."

Selena rapped her fingers on the table. "I really don't have time to deal with you right now." She got to her feet. "Lori, if you're coming with me, you'd better get moving. I'm leaving in ten minutes."

"Hold on to your britches," Lori grumbled as she grabbed a piece of toast and smeared on a chunk of butter.

"You have *ten* minutes." Selena grabbed her purse and headed outside.

Pursing her lips together, Jocelyn stared at Lori with frost in her eyes. Finally, she said, "I don't know what my daughter has planned for this little trip today, but you can be certain it's not going to be pleasant. Selena is too much like her father. Determined. Unpredictable. Maybe even a bit evil. If you want my advice, you'll stay as far away from her as possible."

"Selena's certainly no angel, but evil?" She rolled her eyes at the thought.

Jocelyn leaned back in her chair. "I see you're one of those people who have to learn everything the hard way."

Shrugging, Lori stuffed a chunk of toast in her mouth and washed it down with a swallow of coffee.

Jocelyn scraped back her chair and stood up. "You can't say I didn't warn you."

As Jocelyn headed for the door, Lori called out, "She knows what happened to Kay."

Jocelyn turned back, spat out the word, "Kay." Her lips curled into a sneer. "Why don't you just let that sainted sister of yours rest in peace and get on with your own life?"

Lori's temper started to rise. "For your information, my sister was a wonderful, kind, good-hearted person."

"Spare me the eulogy. I heard enough of that baloney at the funeral."

Lori's eyes widened. "You were there?"

Jocelyn nodded. "In the back."

She shook her head, perplexed. "Why would you go to the funeral of someone you'd never met?"

Jocelyn shrugged. "She was my baby girl's

stepmother."

And Trevor's wife, she started to point out, then thought better of it.

"Truth is, I'd really hoped to bump into Selena. But Derek hustled me out of there so fast, I didn't have a chance to speak to her."

Lori began to speculate about Derek's part in this whole mother/daughter plan to reconnect. What did he hope to gain?

"It probably wasn't the best time to approach her anyway. She was pretty wiped out. Mainly because, her step-mother chose the wrong moment to die, and she missed out on the all-important *party*."

"If you know what's good for you," Jocelyn said, "you'll skip this trip she has planned for the two of you. Trust me, nothing good will come from it."

Lori met her gaze. "I'm afraid I can't do that."

"Then you'll be the one who suffers for it," Jocelyn warned. Then turned and strode away.

Somehow, breakfast had lost its appeal. Lori gulped down another swallow of coffee, then plodded upstairs to change into something more suitable for her lunch date.

By the time she made it outside, eleven minutes had passed. Selena was parked by the front door, engine revving. Lori climbed into the car and, before she even got her seatbelt fastened, Selena gunned the engine, then tore off down the drive.

All her attempts at conversation met with a dead end. Only when Jocelyn's name came up did Selena have anything to say. "Thirty years ago that woman walked out of my father's life. Now for some reason, she thinks she can traipse back into our lives and pick up where she left off." She snorted. "Like that will ever happen."

"I don't think Trevor wants—"

"Who does she think she is anyway?" There was scorn in Selena's voice. "I'm a grown woman with a husband of my own. I don't need her butting into my life."

Lori had few memories of her own mother. Most of what she knew about the fair-haired woman in the locket Kay had worn about her neck came to her second hand—from Kay's stories about her. "I don't think any of us ever outgrows the need for a mother."

Cutting a sideways glance toward Lori, Selena said, "I understand now why she left my father. It was greed—pure and simple. When my father couldn't give her all the luxuries she wanted, she left him for someone who could."

Something didn't ring true about her explanation. "Your father is not exactly a poor man. You have any idea how much beach front property is worth in today's market?"

"It doesn't matter," Selena said. "The land has been in our family for generations. Father would never put it on the market. No matter how strapped he gets for cash."

Selena seemed to drift off to a place where Lori couldn't follow. Every attempt she made at conversation after that met with a wall of silence. Finally, she gave up trying to get any information out of her and turned her attention to the passing scenery.

They were speeding down Highway 90, retracing the route of the Old Spanish Trail. Before long they crossed the bridge into Biloxi, one of the oldest cities in the US, predating even Mobile, or New Orleans. To her left was one of the world's longest man-made beaches, and beyond it, the Mississippi Sound.

A few miles after they'd passed the lighthouse, which was plunked down in the center of the median, Selena took a right. They drove on for several minutes, then Lori asked, "Mind telling me where we're headed?"

"Actually," Selena slid into a parking space, "we're here." She snapped open her seatbelt and slid out of the car.

Lori followed suit, and with quick, smooth steps, followed Selena along the sidewalk to a small, independent bookstore. As they browsed through the bargain bin near the window, Lori wrinkled her brow in puzzlement. "I thought you were taking me to the restaurant where you and Kay had lunch."

"Patience, little sister. You'll understand what we're doing here soon enough."

"I only came with you today because you promised—"

"There." Selena dropped the book she was holding back into the bin and nodded toward the coffee shop across the street.

Lori's stomach rumbled. "Great. I could do with a cup of coffee and a sweet roll about now."

"Don't you ever think about anything, but your stomach?"

"I function better after I've had a few cups of coffee."

"Forget caffeine. See that man coming down the sidewalk?" She herded Lori over to the large, plate glass window. "Does he remind you of anybody?"

Lori's gaze shifted to the man plodding along the sidewalk. Of course, he reminded her of someone—Selena's husband. Confusion settled over her face. "You brought me here to spy on Marc?" She moved away from the window.

"Wait." Selena grabbed her arm. "You're going to miss what I brought you here to see." There was a gleam of triumph in her eyes.

Despite her good intentions, Lori's gaze drifted back

to the sidewalk. She saw Marc head inside the coffee shop and stop at a booth near the front. A short, dark-headed woman stood up to greet him. After a quick hug, she sat back down, and he slid into the booth across from her.

Lori's face grew hot. She peeled her gaze away from the pair in the coffee shop and glared at Selena. "Is this why you brought me here? So we could watch your husband have breakfast with—"

"I brought you here," Selena interrupted, "to prove to you that Marc was never the angel you thought he was."

There had to be a reasonable explanation for Marc's actions, Lori thought. He wasn't the kind of man who would cheat on his wife. At least, she didn't think he was. "Who's the woman?"

Selena shrugged. "Does it matter?"

"Not to me," Lori said, arching her brows. "But it seems to me you'd want to know who the woman hanging out with you husband is. Especially since she's probably half your age."

Selena raised her hand as if to slap her. Then, regained control of her emotions and let it fall to her side. "You let me worry about my husband."

As if sensing a disturbance brewing in her quiet, little shop, the silver-headed shop owner hurried down the aisle, dust wand flapping. "Is there a problem, ladies?"

Selena turned around and glared at the woman. "Everything is fine," she snapped.

The shop owner halted in her tracks, looking uncertain. "Uh . . . well. Let me know if you need anything." She went back to her dusting, but didn't stray far.

Something didn't add up here. The Selena she grew up with wasn't big on sharing. Not her toys. Not her clothes. And certainly not her man. "Why aren't you upset about seeing Marc with another woman?"

"Because, unlike you, I'm confident in my ability to hold onto my man. Marc might be attracted to another woman from time to time, but in the end, he always comes back to me." Her voice dropped a notch. "And always will."

Lori's eyes narrowed. "So, all this good marriage stuff was a sham?"

"On the contrary," Selena said. "There's a bond between Marc and me that can never be broken. No matter who tries to come between us."

So that's what this little excursion was about. Selena wanted to send a clear message—Marc wasn't the kind of man to leave his wife. What Selena didn't understand, probably wasn't capable of understanding, was Lori had a strong sense of right and wrong that would never allow her to destroy the bond between a husband and wife. No matter how damaged the relationship might be.

"What's this little charade got to do with Kay?" she asked.

Selena shrugged. "Nothing. I just thought I'd set you straight about a few things."

Fueled by anger, Lori went on the attack. "I know you took Kay out for lunch shortly before she died, and something about that trip upset her." She folded her arms across her chest. "And I don't intend to leave here until you tell me what happened."

"Oh that." A smug look flitted across Selena's face. "I merely opened her eyes to something she'd been trying to ignore."

"Such as?"

Selena's eyes narrowed. "It's none of your business."

"Of course, it's my business. She was my sister. And

somebody murdered her. Quiet possibly, because of something you dragged her into that day."

Selena rolled her eyes. "When are you going to get it through your head—nobody murdered your sister. She fell down the stairs. It was an unfortunate accident, but it happened. You'll just have to find a way to deal with it."

"What about this Grant family secret? Maybe it's mixed up with her death somehow."

"Trust me—it isn't."

Lori's chin inched up. "How can you be so sure?"

"Because . . . " Selena jacked up one shoulder. "I just know, that's how."

Lori took a moment to gather her patience. "You said you opened her eyes to something she'd been trying to ignore. What was she trying to ignore?"

Selena started to say something, then spun away and strode down the aisle. Lori caught up with her by the front door. "You knew she'd had several miscarriages." She didn't bother to hide her anger. "Why would you deliberately upset her?"

"It's not my fault she kept miscarrying."

How many times had Selena used the same excuse? It's not my fault?

"But you could have been a little nicer to her," Lori said. "Not dumped more headaches in her lap."

"For your information"—those cat-green eyes narrowed—"I was trying to help Kay, not hurt her."

"Right," Lori said. "How could I forget? You were always so good to Kay. When we were growing up, you never caused her a moment of grief. That was some *other* step-daughter."

"Okay. So I was no angel. That doesn't mean I'd deliberately try to hurt her."

Lori zeroed in on the word deliberately. "But you *did* hurt her."

Selena drew in a breath before answering. "Maybe."

Lori waited for Selena to elaborate. Eventually, she obliged. "While we were having lunch that day, I might've mentioned seeing Father there the week before with another woman. And she shouldn't be surprised if they came strolling through the door any moment."

Lori tried to tamp down the fury that was growing inside her. "Of all the pig-headed things you've done. This has to be one of the—"

The silver-headed storeowner was back. "Ladies, I'll have to ask you to keep your voices down, or vacate the premises."

"Leave. Us. Alone." The look Selena shot the woman sent her scurrying toward the cash register. Turning her attention back to Lori, she said, "How was I supposed to know Kay was going to have a melt-down?"

Lori shook her head in disbelief. "You told a pregnant woman that you saw her husband meeting another woman for lunch, and you didn't think it might upset her?"

"Okay, so maybe I wanted to shake her up a little. Make her pay for all the nasty things she was thinking about my marriage."

Something occurred to Lori. "How did you know Trevor and this woman would be there?"

Her face reddened. "I overheard him talking to her."

Lori gave her a knowing look.

"He put her on speaker-phone." She defended her action. "What was I supposed to do—cover my ears?"

"Did you bother to find out who this woman is? Or how she knows Trevor?"

"Do I look like a dummy? Of course I checked her out. She's a loan officer at Father's bank." She paused a beat, then added, "A very, pretty loan officer."

Lori took a moment to gather her patience. "Did it ever occur to you that your father might be having some cash flow problems? That he might be trying to get a loan from the bank to tide him over? That his lunch date might just be a business meeting?"

"I suppose it's possible. But"—her chin jutted up—"I didn't force Kay to march out of there without talking to him."

Lori sighed. The concept of taking responsibility for one's actions was a totally foreign concept to Selena. "I think we're done here," she said, then stepped outside into the warm sunshine.

CHAPTER EIGHTEEN

On the drive home, Selena remained silent, wrapped up in her own thoughts. Lori was glad. She needed time to process what she had just witnessed. The idea of Marc cheating on his wife was hard to believe. He wasn't the type. The woman she saw him with was probably a friend. Or a business associate.

She didn't want to believe it. Except—the woman had seemed awful friendly.

Which led to an even more disturbing thought: a person could change a lot in seven years. What if she had put her trust in the wrong man?

When they reached the house, Selena let Lori out by the front door. "I'll see you later. I really need to put in a few hours at the store. I hate the way that imbecile I hired last week arranged that last batch of items I brought in. I knew I should've taken care of it myself."

Wrapped in a cloud of depression, Lori plodded upstairs to her room and plopped down on the wicker sofa. Half an hour later, Lou Ann, who believed food was the cure for everything, bumped on the door. Without waiting for an answer, she sashayed inside with a tray loaded with a fruit salad, a peanut butter and jelly sandwich, and a large glass of milk.

Though she wasn't hungry, Lori knew skipping lunch wasn't an option. Not when Lou Ann stood over her the whole time, clucking like a mother hen until she had eaten the last bite. "Now, park that skinny behind of yours in bed and rest. Miss Annabel's orders."

"I'm not an invalid, you know."

Lou Ann crossed her arms and glared at Lori. "Best do what I say."

Deciding to humor the woman, she crawled into bed, then closed her eyes and tried to relax.

"That's better," Lou Ann said. "You just take yourself a nice, long nap so I can tell Miss Annabel she don't have to worry about you no more."

Lori's eyes popped back open. "You tell her she doesn't need to worry about me. I'm perfectly fine."

Ignoring Lori's comment, Lou Ann went on, "You know, Miss Annabel ain't as spry as she used to be." She rocked her head up and down, then added, "That's something you young people need to keep in mind."

Realizing Lou Ann probably knew more about what was going on in this house than the rest of the family combined, she rolled over on her side and said, "Lou Ann, I'm sure you must have noticed that Kay wasn't herself these last few months. Any idea what was bothering her?"

Turning away, the old woman began to tidy the room. "I find it ain't too healthy to go poking you nose into other people's business. Especially not with the people who sign your paycheck."

Lori hopped up and strode across the room. "Come on, Lou Ann. You were always the first one to know when Selena and I were up to mischief. You had to know something was bothering Kay."

"I might've noticed something." She gathered up a couple of blouses Lori had left on one of the chairs in the sitting area and shuffled toward the closet. "Miss Kay seemed a mite jumpy these last few weeks. At first, I thought it was because of the baby." She slid the blouses onto hangers. "That she was scared of losing another one. Then I got to noticing how she nearly jumped out of her skin every time anyone got close to her. That seemed real unusual. Miss Kay's always been the huggy-feely type."

Lori felt her excitement grow. "Did she seem that way with everyone, or with someone in particular?"

Lou Ann moved to the bed and began smoothing the spread. Lori trailed after her, helping her fluff the pillows.

"No one in particular, that I can recall," Lou Ann said. "She pretty much got twitchy whenever anybody got close to her. Kind of like she was expecting something bad to happen. Only . . . that don't make no sense. Who'd want to hurt someone who was always so good to everybody?"

Someone who saw her as a threat, perhaps.

"Did Kay ever mention anything to you about someone playing tricks on her?"

Lou Ann's gaze riveted to her. "No. And I'd better not find out that someone . . . " Her words died out when she realized it was a little late for threats. She crossed her arms. "Didn't I tell you to plant that skinny behind of yours in that bed?"

Climbing meekly back into bed, Lori pretended to sleep. Her plan was to hop back up the minute Lou Ann left the room. Only, while she waited, her eyes began to grow heavy . . .

When she woke up, nearly an hour had passed. Though she felt more rested than she had in days, she knew time was pressing in. Today was Wednesday. Monday she had to return to her life in Texas. But how could she leave until she knew the truth about Kay's death?

Already, the clues were growing dim. Soon they would fizzle out altogether. It was time to crank up her investigation. But first, she needed to confront Marc about this mystery woman he'd met for lunch and make sure he could still be trusted.

***

Thirty minutes later, she stormed into Marc's restaurant, ready for battle. She found him in the kitchen overseeing a delivery. From the look on her face, he must have sensed her need to talk. After barking out a few orders to his staff, he took her arm and steered her outside to the deck, where tables had already been set with silverware and napkins.

A slight breeze ruffled his hair as he selected a table near the railing. A couple of boats chugged past in the bright sunlight headed for the Sound, and probably on to one of the barrier islands. A young boy waved from the deck of the larger boat. Smiling, Marc returned his wave.

Now that the time had come to speak her mind, Lori's courage faltered. She was relieved when Marc took the lead. "Kind of reminds me of all those times we spent running back and forth to the islands." There was a hint of wistfulness in his voice.

"Does Trevor still own the Amber Wave?" She played along, acting as if her visit was nothing more than a social call. "Or did he sell it and get something newer?"

"Are you kidding?" Marc said, with fake shock. "Trevor would never sell the Amber Wave. She's like a member of the family. This past winter, he pulled her into dry dock and had some work done on her. Now, she's good as new."

Lori sighed, remembering all the fun she'd had aboard the Amber Wave. Hours of drifting around the islands, wading ashore to collect shells and pieces of driftwood, munching delicious goodies from those enormous picnic baskets Lou Ann had packed for them. "That's one of the things I miss most about this place. Long, lazy days on the water."

"Then I'll have to speak to Trevor about taking us out before you leave. I'm sure he'd jump at any excuse to get out on the water."

"I'd like that."

They sat there a while longer, admiring the boats chugging past, their owners sometimes honking their horns in greeting, sometimes only giving a quick wave. With a sigh of regret, Lori finally opened her mouth and shattered the peace they'd enjoyed. "I saw you this morning," she said, then studied his face for any hint of discomfort.

His brows knotted together in puzzlement.

"At the coffee shop," she said.

He jerked his elbows off the table and sat up straighter. A shield came down over his over his face.

"We were across the street," she explained, "at the book store."

"Hold on a minute." His eyes narrowed. "We being . . .?"

She began to squirm about under his intense gaze. "Selena and I."

"You expect me to believe the two of you just happened to be across the street from the coffee shop. Together. At the same time."

"Well, not exactly."

"Let me see if I can figure this out. Selena came up with this great idea, talked you into going off with her, and you meekly followed along like some dumb animal, knowing she was leading you into trouble."

Lori resented the implication that she'd allowed Selena to manipulate her. Even if it happened to be true. She went on the offensive. "Don't try to make this about me. Who was that woman we saw you with?"

He seemed to debate with himself whether to answer. "Okay," he finally said, "but what I'm about to tell you goes no further than the two of us. Agreed?"

Lori thought about it a moment, then nodded.

"She happens to be an old friend of mine." At her

hoot of disbelief, he hurried on, "Let me finish. She also happens to be Trevor's accountant. After you told me about the conversation you overheard between Jocelyn and Trevor, I decided to do a little checking." He paused, cleared his throat, then went on, "Guess it's a good thing I did. Seems there's been a few suspicious items on the books this past year."

"Well," she said, when he wasn't forthcoming with details, "don't keep me in suspense."

"For the past year Trevor's been sending a check every month to a JCG Enterprises in Atlanta."

She hunched her shoulders. "So?"

"So, there are no invoices on file for this company that Cindy could find. When she asked Trevor about it, he told her to list it as a consultant fee. Being the stickler for details that she is, Cindy made a few phone calls and discovered the company is owned by—"

There was a gnawing ache in the pit of Lori's stomach. "Jocelyn Grant," she said before he could finish.

He pointed his index finger at her. "Bingo."

"How much money are we talking about?"

"Each check was made out for five thousand dollars." He did some quick figuring. "Around sixty grand, I'd say."

Lori gave a soft whistle. "That's a lot of money. I wonder if Kay knew about it?"

"Since Kay called Trevor's secretary a few weeks ago wanting the phone number for JCG Enterprises in Atlanta, I'd have to say—yes, she knew."

Lori frowned. "Guess that explains why Trevor was sleeping in the study."

"Probably."

"Of course," Lori said, "that still doesn't explain why anyone would want to kill Kay. She had nothing to do with his business."

Trevor fiddled with his shirt collar. "Unless she decided to confront the person who was blackmailing her husband."

While Lori was considering the matter, the chunky waitress she'd met a few days ago came bustling outside, carrying two tall glasses of iced tea. "Thought you could use something cold to drink, as hot as it's getting to be."

After thanking her, they settled back, resumed their perusal of the river traffic, each lost in their own speculations.

Lori finally broke the silence. "I wonder how Selena knew you'd be meeting Trevor's accountant this morning?"

Marc shook his head. "Maybe she overheard me on the phone with Cindy last night."

"So I guess Selena doesn't really think you're having an affair?"

There was no hesitation in his reply. "She has no reason to."

She searched his face for some signs of deception. Relaxed, when she couldn't detect any.

"More than likely," he said, "she wanted to arouse *your* suspicions. Make you feel you couldn't trust me, so you'd run back to Texas with your tail between your legs like a hurt puppy."

Which would solve Selena's biggest problem, Lori thought.

Again, they returned to their perusal of the river traffic. Finally, Lori said, "You think Jocelyn is capable of murder?"

Marc seemed to take her question seriously. "Truthfully. I have no idea."

CHAPTER NINETEEN

After leaving the restaurant, Lori drove back to Oakwood. As she pulled up in front of the house, the door flew open and Lou Ann clumped down the steps, a green dishtowel clutched in her hand. "Thank goodness you're back."

Her high-pitched tone set alarm bells clanging. "What's wrong?"

"It's Miss Annabel," Lou Ann said, between puffs of breath. "She looks awful. Just awful."

Remembering the heart attack Annabel had had a few years back, Lori said, "Did you try to get hold of her doctor? Or Trevor?"

Lou Ann nodded. "I was just dialing Trevor's number when I heard you drive up. Since she's been asking for you, I thought I best get out here and send you on up. Maybe you can calm her down."

Lori slid an arm around Lou Ann's shoulders and steered her toward the door. Lou Ann jerked away and gave a disgusted snort. "You never mind about me. I can take care of myself. You just get up them stairs and see what you can do for Miss Annabel. Like I told you, she ain't been well these past few years. She can't take no more of this foolishness that's been going on around here."

"I'm sure everything will be fine," Lori tried to sound comforting. "But just to be on the safe side, maybe you'd better call Trevor and ask him to swing by the house."

Lori ran upstairs and rapped lightly on Annabel's

door before entering. Today, the drapes were still drawn, blocking out the morning light, giving the room a gloomy appearance. She found Annabel huddled along one end of the sofa and knelt beside her.

Lou Ann's warning hadn't prepared her for how bad Annabel looked. Gone was the well-groomed woman she'd always known. In her place was a stranger with long, knotted hair; pasty, white skin; and the dark-smudged eyes of someone who hadn't been getting enough sleep."

"Hang on, Annabel. I'm going to call an ambulance. We need to get you to the hospital."

"No." Annabel clutched at her hand. "I'm not having another heart attack. I know what that feels like. And I'm not going to any hospital."

Lori saw determination in the older woman's face and gave in. "Okay, but let's get you back in bed."

There was a frantic look in Annabel's eyes. "I need to talk to you first."

"We can talk," Lori said firmly, "after we get you tucked into bed." She helped the older woman up and got her settled in the queen-sized bed. "Now, what was it you wanted to talk to me about?"

"I know what I'm going to tell you may sound crazy." She grabbed Lori's arm. "But please hear me out."

"Of course," Lori said, keeping her voice soft.

"Sometimes I have these feelings—kind of warnings, actually," Annabel said. "The first time it happened, the boys were young and I was on my way to the store. Suddenly, I had this strange urge to turn around and rush home. I tried to ignore the feeling at first, but it grew so strong that I finally gave up on the idea of shopping and headed back home. I'm so grateful I did. Trevor had gone for a swim and nearly drowned. Thank goodness, his father reached him in time.

Otherwise . . . " The old woman studied Lori's face, as if trying to gage her reaction.

Knowing she had to say something, Lori said, "That's . . . interesting."

Annabel frowned, as if not approving of her answer. "I'm not making this up," she insisted.

"I'm sure you're not." Lori tried to erase all doubt from her voice.

Satisfied with her response, Annabel went on, "This time it was different. More like a dream." Her eyes drifted shut in remembrance. "I saw you lying in the sand, wearing this pretty blue dress. At first, I thought you were napping. But when I tried to wake you, I realized you weren't asleep"—her voice dropped to a whisper—"you were dead."

Despite her skepticism, a shiver scooted up Lori's spine. "Hey, it was only a dream." She tried to sound reassuring. "See, I'm right here. And I'm perfectly fine."

Annabel's eyes popped open. Her face had taken on a feverish glow. "But what if this is another one of those premonitions, or whatever you want to call them? That would mean . . . you might be in serious danger."

"Don't worry." Lori tucked the covers around her. "It was only a dream."

The old woman's eyes had taken on a wild look. "But what if it was a warning?"

"Then thanks to you, I'll be extra cautious."

"Yes. Yes." She sounded deflated. "I suppose that's all you can do. Whatever is going to happen, will happen."

Lori leaned over and kissed her wrinkled cheek. "I'm going to run downstairs and have Lou Ann brew up some of that nice, herbal tea you love so much."

"That's very kind of you, dear," Annabel said, and closed her eyes.

In the kitchen, Lori found Lou Ann slumped at the table, an untouched cup of coffee in front of her. Once she explained about Annabel's dream, Lou Ann seemed somewhat relieved.

"So you don't think we need to call an ambulance?"

Lori shook her head and set to work filling the kettle with water. "I think she's just tired from not sleeping well, that's all."

Lou Ann pushed up from the table and muscled her aside. "Here, let me do that. You get back up them stairs and sit with Miss Annabel a while. Read her some of that poetry stuff she likes. I'll bring up the tea when it's ready."

For almost an hour, Lori sat at Annabel's side, reading aloud from the poems by Elizabeth Barrett Browning. The door opened twice while she was there. Once when Lou Ann brought in tea and cookies, then again when Trevor popped in to check on his mother. By then Annabel was nearly asleep. Lori motioned him away and went on reading. Ten minutes later, she closed the book and crept from the room.

She found Trevor in the kitchen and slid into the chair across from him. Since Lou Ann had already clued him in about Annabel's premonition, there was little else she could tell him.

He glanced at his watch. "How long do you think she'll sleep? I have an appointment in town that I really need to keep."

Lori urged him to go take care of his business; she'd call him if anything changed. "She'll probably sleep most of the afternoon anyway."

As he pushed back from the table, she noticed his bloodshot eyes. She opened her mouth to suggest he could use a nap himself, then realized he wouldn't appreciate the suggestion.

After he was gone, restlessness drove her outside to

the patio. The sun beamed down, making the metal furniture too hot to sit on, so she found a cool spot under a magnolia tree and plopped down. She toyed with the idea of taking a walk, but after Annabel's premonition—if that's what it was—she decided it was best not to tempt fate.

Then it occurred to her, with Trevor tied up in town, she could plunder through his study without fear of being caught. She might even get lucky and find Kay's missing locket. Or, even better, her diary.

Not that she suspected Trevor of taking them.

Still, it wouldn't hurt to check.

CHAPTER TWENTY

Trevor's desk was one of those massive, oak pieces with two drawers on either side, connected by a shallow drawer across the middle. Lori began her search with the center drawer. It contained the usual assortment of office supplies: pens, pencils, a stapler. She moved on to the drawers on the left, where she found nothing of importance.

The drawers on the right, however, were another story. In the top one, underneath a pile of papers was a handgun. She was so stunned, she couldn't tear her gaze away. Then a surge of anger rocked through her veins. How could Trevor be so careless? What if Amber needed a pencil, or piece of paper, and came across the gun? She might be injured, or worst yet—killed.

She slammed the drawer shut and jerked open the bottom one. Thankfully, it contained no firearms, only files. Most of them seemed to deal with household matters; others, real estate dealings. She flipped through a few, but found nothing of importance. She was ready to give up when she spotted a leather notebook tucked between the last two folders.

She slipped it from its hiding place and thumbed through a few pages. When she realized it was a woman's diary, a tingle of excitement shot through every cell of her body. She scanned through one of the entries: "Everything is going well. I've never been so happy. Yesterday, I found out about the baby. I'm not sure what to do. I'm afraid that if he finds out the truth, he might kill me.

The thud of footsteps drawing closer finally penetrated the fog in her brain. She jammed the diary back in the drawer and darted across the room to the bookcase. Seconds later, Trevor sailed through the door. Catching sight of her, he came to an abrupt stop.

She grabbed a book off the top shelf. "I thought I'd find something to read to Annabel when she wakes up."

Accepting her explanation at face value, he continued toward his desk.

Going for that just-making-conversation tone, she added, "I thought you had an appointment in town."

"I do." He deposited his briefcase on the desk and snapped it open. "I was on my way there when I realized I'd left behind one of the files I needed." He pulled open the right bottom drawer, grabbed the forgotten folder, and stuffed it into his briefcase.

Fear began to pulse through her body. Had she put the diary back in the exact spot she'd found it? Though she continued to flip through the pages of the book she was holding, she kept darting glances his way, watching for any sign that something was amiss.

Satisfied he had everything, he started to nudge the drawer shut. Then changed his mind, reached back inside, and grabbed the diary. He tossed it on top of his other paperwork, said, "See you later," and headed off to his meeting.

Feeling exhausted, she shuffled to the nearest chair and sagged down. If she'd had more time to examine the diary, she might've figured out who it belonged to. One thing was certain, it wasn't Kay's. Her handwriting was large and loopy; this writing was much smaller and had a leftward slant.

She wasn't sure how long she sat there, staring at the walls, trying to figure out her next move, before she became aware of voices in the hallway.

"Look, I'm only asking for a couple thousand

bucks," she heard Derek say. "Don't tell me you can't spare that."

"A couple of thousand," Jocelyn said. "You've got a serious problem and you need to do something about it. If Trevor ever finds out—"

"He won't."

"Selena might let something slip."

"I can handle Selena. She worships the ground I walk on."

There was a long pause. "Okay. Drive me to the bank and I'll get the money," Jocelyn said. "But this is the last time I'm going to bail you out. You screw up again and you're on your own."

"Thanks, babe. I owe you."

"Don't worry. I'll be sure to collect."

Lori waited a few minutes, then trudged outside. Forgetting Annabel's warning, she strolled along the beach, replaying the conversation in her head. Did Derek have an addiction problem? To drugs? Alcohol? She remembered the envelope he'd handed Mr. Stevens at Kay's wake and decided a gambling addiction made the most sense.

Since Derek was headed to the bank, it seemed like the perfect time to check out his place. Reversing course, she trotted toward the small cottage, which sat behind the main house, off to the right side of the property.

Tucked under a massive oak, the house was small, no bigger than a one-bedroom apartment. Green shutters stood out against a white background. To be safe, she knocked on the front door. There was no answer, so she tried the knob. It was locked.

Refusing to give up, she walked past a bed of ferns around to the back of the house, where she might have better luck. She tried the knob, and found it unlocked.

The door opened to a postage-sized kitchen. It didn't

take long to search through the handful of cabinets. The only thing she learned was Derek liked his booze. Lots of booze. And the man didn't own a decent set of dishes.

The living room contained a sofa, a large screen TV, a couple of armchairs, and a coffee table. No pictures on the wall, no knickknacks, no clutter of any kind. Not even an ashtray.

Next item on her agenda was the bedroom. On the nightstand, she found a photograph of Derek, Trevor, and Jocelyn during their teenage years in a cheap metal frame. Which seemed an odd, decorative choice for a grown man. The drawers underneath were completely empty.

She moved on to the dresser. Found nothing of importance there. Shifted her attention to the closet. It was crammed with expensive clothes and shoes, but nothing that interested her. She turned away, ready to admit defeat, when she caught sight of something shiny under the edge of the bed.

She leaned down and fished out the object, which turned out to be the missing locket. Tears misted her eyes as she ran a finger over the rose etched on its surface. She clicked open the latch and found her mother's picture still intact.

One by one, questions began to tumble through her mind. What was Derek doing with Kay's locket? Had he stolen it from her room? Or was he hiding it for someone else?

What about Kay's diary? Had he stolen that, too?

She got down on her knees to conduct a more thorough search. Found nothing but dust bunnies. She stood up, considered the situation a moment, then ran a hand between the mattress and box springs. Grew excited when she felt the hard edges of a book.

When she pulled it out, she found her sister's

handwriting inside and began to thumb through the pages. Most of the entries weren't all that interesting: how Kay had felt about being pregnant, where she had gone and what she'd done each day. Certainly, nothing worth stealing.

Then why take it?

To intimidate her, make her seem paranoid, or use her to get to Trevor?

She hated leaving Kay's diary and locket behind, but if she took them, Derek would know his cottage had been searched, so she put the items back where she'd found them.

She was on her way to do another sweep of the living room when she heard voices outside the cottage. She barely made it to the kitchen before the front door open. Her heart was thumping like a rock band as she crept toward the back door.

Her hand was on the back doorknob when Jocelyn's voice penetrated her blood-deprived brain. "I can't believe you could be so stupid. What were you thinking? No, don't bother to answer. You weren't thinking."

"Give it a rest, woman," Derek replied. "How could I know Selena would be there. It's not like she has any business at Mr. Stevens' office."

"Then why was she there?"

"She claimed she was there to sell him a raffle ticket for some club she belongs to."

"But you don't believe her," Jocelyn said.

There was a pause. "We're talking about Selena, the Princess of Devious."

"Right," Jocelyn said. "You told me that she's not exactly truthful, but I don't understand why she'd lie about something so trivial."

"It's not that she sets out to lie," Derek defended his niece.

"Yeah," Jocelyn replied, "I've heard that one before."

"Have I ever lied to you?"

Jocelyn ignored the question. "Maybe she knows about the money."

"I don't see how," Derek said. "Hey, you want something to drink? I have some bourbon in the kitchen."

That was Lori's cue to get moving. She shot through the door, eased it closed behind her, and didn't stop moving until she reached the beach.

By the time she returned to the house, Trevor's car was parked out front. She went looking for him and found him in his study. He glanced up from the papers he was working on. "Everything all right?" There was a note of concern in his voice.

She realized he probably thought she was here about his mother. "Don't worry," she said quickly. "Annabel's fine. She's upstairs resting."

"Good." He leaned back in his chair. "Look, I hope you don't believe all that nonsense about Mother having premonitions."

She wandered across the room and plopped down on the sofa. "I try to keep an open mind about such things."

Trevor got up and joined her on the sofa. "Is something bothering you? You seem a little distracted."

She wouldn't meet his gaze. "What could I possibly be worried about?"

"Any number of things, I would imagine." His tone was soft, gentle, an invitation for her to unburden herself.

She decided to give him a chance to make things right and told him about finding Kay's locket and diary in Derek's cottage.

He was quiet for a moment. "Who else have you told

about this?"

"Nobody."

"Let's keep it that way. The fewer people who know about this the better."

She studied him. "What are you planning to do about it?"

He sighed. "For the moment, nothing. I need time to figure out the best way to handle the situation."

She jumped up off the couch. "Maybe I should just talk to Derek myself."

His head snapped up. "You need to stay away from Derek. He can be—"

"Dangerous," she said.

"I was going to say, temperamental."

She glared at him. "We both know you have no intention of confronting Derek. You've probably known all along he was the one harassing Kay, the one snooping through my room, and you did nothing about it." A razor-sharp pain tore through her temple.

"What does he have on you?" she asked, when the pain finally eased.

Trevor strode back to his desk, sat down, and fiddled with the papers laid out before him. "Look, things are . . . complicated. I don't think Mother's health can take any more excitement. You saw her this afternoon. She isn't well."

She marched over and braced her arms on his desk. "I don't see what Annabel has to do with this. My sister is dead. And I'm pretty sure someone in this house killed her."

He grabbed another folder from his briefcase and began to leaf through its contents. "Like I told you before, Kay's death was an accident."

It took all the strength she could muster to tamp down the fire raging inside. When she finally had her emotions under control, she said, "Something is very wrong in this house. And I think you know what it is. What I don't understand is why you're not doing something about it."

He looked up from his papers. "You need to back off and let me handle this." His voice was harsh and unrelenting. "I can't protect you if you won't listen to me."

"I don't need protecting," she said. "I need the truth."

He met her gaze. "And I promise, you'll get it. In due time."

CHAPTER TWENTY-ONE

On Saturday morning, Annabel was more like her old self. Though in good spirits, she didn't venture far from bed. It was just as well, since Lori wasn't sure how she'd react to Marc's suggestion they make a run out to the islands.

The rest of the family seemed excited about the trip. The men quickly set off to prepare the boat, while Selena and Lori helped Lou Ann pack a lunch. In less than an hour, the women were headed for the marina in Selena's Olds. Lori road shotgun, while Amber and Jocelyn shared the back seat.

As soon as they pulled into the parking lot, Derek and Marc hustled over to help unload the car. It wasn't long until they were bouncing along over open waters. Overhead, the skies were a clear blue, not a storm cloud in sight. A steady wind pounded their bodies, causing their clothing to flap about in the breeze. Now and then, a wave would splash over the bow, coating their faces in a salty mist.

As they drew near the island, Trevor hoisted the motor up and glided into shore. In tandem, Derek and Marc hopped overboard and dragged the boat closer to shore. Sliding into the knee-deep water, Trevor lifted Amber from the boat and deposited her on shore, then went back to help unload all the beach paraphernalia.

Instead of relaxing on shore with the others, Marc and Derek decided to try their luck fishing. They climbed back into the boat and set out for deeper water. Not into the sunbathing scene, Trevor marched off to explore the island, leaving the ladies free to arrange their beach towels along the shore and work on their tans.

It didn't take long to realize Amber was too antsy to lie in the sun doing nothing, so Lori slipped on her pale blue beach robe and offered to take her beach combing. When the pair grew tired of collecting shells and chunks of driftwood, they dumped their loot onto the hard, packed sand near the water's edge and sat down to sort through their treasures.

Before long, the two were hard at work building an elaborate sandcastle, complete with moat and draw bridge. Now and then, a sad look would flit across Amber's face, making Lori wonder if the girl was thinking of her mother.

Once their sandcastle was finished, Lori said, "Want to collect more driftwood?"

Amber shook her head, sending her ponytail swinging. "Maybe later." That sad look flicked across her face again.

"How about this," Lori said, jumping to her feet, "let's write messages in the sand." Without waiting for a response, Lori padded off in search of a good, strong stick.

Sitting cross-legged in the sand, Amber stayed where she was and watched as Lori carved giant letters in the damp sand. After awhile, curiosity got the best of her. She trotted over to read the message: "Lori Reynolds was here."

The girl grinned, took the stick Lori held out, then began to carve out her own message: "Amber rules." Once she was done, she hurled the stick as far as she could into the water.

Agreeing they needed fuel, the twosome headed back to join the others. As they walked along the water's edge, Amber said, "Sometimes I really miss my mommy."

Lori sighed. "I miss her, too."

"At least it wasn't your fault she died," the girl mumbled.

Lori stopped walking. "What did you say?"

Amber lowered her head and stared at the grainy sand. "If I'd put my dolls away like I was supposed to, Mommy wouldn't have tripped over them and fallen down the stairs."

This is the first Lori had heard about any dolls left on the stairs. Maybe this was what had put that fear in Trevor's eyes. The thought his daughter might be blamed for her mother's death.

But that would mean, Kay's death really was an accident.

Which she didn't believe. Her sister was afraid of someone in that house. Enough so that she wanted to send her daughter away to protect her.

And what about this family secret Selena had mentioned? And the possible blackmail money Trevor was forking out? Something was definitely out of whack in this household.

But what did any of it have to do with Kay's murder?

Parking the matter in the think-about-it-later part of her brain, Lori reached over and put an arm around Amber's shoulders. "Honey, what happened to your mother wasn't your fault." She couldn't bring herself to add the words, "It was an accident," no matter how comforting the words might've been.

Tears leaked down Amber's face. "I thought I put away my dolls. Honest. I don't remember leaving them on the stairs. But I must have. How else did they get there?"

She gazed into those big, brown eyes so like Kay's. "Honey, no one blames you for what happened."

She pulled away. "Yes, they do."

Lori clamped her hands on Amber's shoulders. "That's nonsense. Everybody knows you loved your mother, that you'd never do anything to hurt her."

Amber's chin jutted out. "Selena thinks so."

Lori was too shocked to reply right away. "Don't be silly," she said, when her voice returned. "Selena knows you would never hurt anyone."

"She thinks I left my dolls out on purpose," Amber insisted. "I heard her talking to Uncle Derek. She told him that Mommy tripped over them. That's why she fell down the stairs. She said that if I hadn't been so careless, Mommy would still be alive."

If Selena had been within sparring distance, Lori would have knocked her out cold. She took Amber's face in her hands. "Listen to me, young lady," she said sternly. "What happened to you mother was not your fault. Do you hear me? If your mother knew you were blaming yourself for what happened, she'd be very angry with you."

Throwing herself against Lori, Amber began to sob uncontrollably. Lori patted her back and made soothing noises until the tears trickled out. Then, out of nowhere, Trevor appeared. He searched Lori's face, looking for a clue about his daughter's unhappiness. Lori shook her head and mouthed the word, "Later."

He seemed to get the message. Leaning down, he said, "How would my favorite girl like to go for a walk with her dear, old dad?"

Lori wiped away Amber's tears with the corner of her beach robe. "I'm sure she'd love that."

As they strolled away, she watched Trevor sling an arm around Amber's shoulders. Unbidden, Selena's words popped into her head: "I know he hates me." As hard as it was for her to admit, maybe Selena was right. She searched her memory, trying to recall an image of

Trevor throwing his arm across Selena's shoulders, and came up empty.

Deep in thought, Lori strolled along the water's edge back to sunbathe-central. She approached her old, childhood playmate with mixed feelings. As her shadow fell across Selena, her pseudo-sister lifted the straw hat from her face and peered up. "Oh, it's you," she said, and promptly let the hat fall back into place.

"You might as well sit down." Jocelyn motioned toward the boat, which was anchored a good piece off shore. "No telling how long they'll be out there."

Lori slipped off her robe and stuffed it into her bag. She arranged her beach towel next to Selena's and plopped down. She lazed there, enjoying the toasty warmth of the sun, watching the two men aboard the boat. Once again, Derek reeled in his line, a muffled curse letting them know how he'd fared.

Jocelyn laughed. "That man never did have any patience."

"That probably explains why he's traveled around so much," Lori said.

Jocelyn frowned. "I don't believe that was the reason."

When Jocelyn failed to offer an explanation for her statement, Selena pushed the straw hat off her face and propped herself up on one elbow. "Well, go on. I'd like to know why Uncle Derek never stayed in one place long enough to put down any roots."

Jocelyn's glance shifted from her daughter to Lori. "It was just a simple misunderstanding between brothers."

When Jocelyn failed to elaborate, Selena said, "What kind of misunderstanding?"

"I wasn't privy to all the details," she said, looking away.

Sure you weren't, Lori thought. *And I'm the Queen*

of England. And if you believe that, I have a plot of swampland to sell you that'll make you rich beyond your wildest dreams.

"Come on," Selena said. "You don't really expect us to believe you didn't know what was going on. Not when you lived in the same house with them." A frown puckered her face. "At least, I assume Uncle Derek was living at Oakwood then. Father hasn't exactly been forthcoming on the subject."

Jocelyn was slow in replying. "He was." She seemed to debate with herself how much to say. "Your father and Derek fought a lot. One day, I guess Derek just had enough. He packed his bags and left."

"Where did he go?" Selena asked.

Jocelyn's gaze fastened on Derek as he reeled in his line. "He sent Annabel a post card from Costa Rica. After that, I think he wandered around awhile."

"Good old, Daddy," Selena was quick to condemn. "Always the loyal family man."

"I wouldn't be too hard on him," Jocelyn said. "Trevor had plenty of reason for what he did." She closed her eyes and sighed. "Plenty of reason."

"That's no excuse for the way Father behaved," Selena said. "Someday he's going to have to pay for how he treated Uncle Derek."

The sound of a motor starting up put an end to their discussion. It appeared the men had had enough fishing for the day. They puttered into shore and anchored the boat. Between them they came ashore carrying a large cooler.

"Sorry," Derek said. "I guess we forgot to unload the cooler with all the drinks." He retrieved a couple of cans of soda from the ice. "Anybody thirsty?"

Jocelyn eagerly accepted the diet drink he held out. "You're a lifesaver." She popped open the top and took a big gulp.

For the next few minutes, they sat around sipping sodas, listening to tales of the day's fishing woes. After awhile, Jocelyn got to her feet and slipped a lavender robe over her lavender, one-piece swimsuit. "I need to stretch my legs a bit. Anyone care to join me?" Her gaze settled on Derek.

Taking his cue, Derek scrambled to his feet. "I guess I can't let you wander off alone. No telling what kind of dangerous creatures you might run into." He nodded at Marc. "Don't go eating all the food up while we're gone."

"Now that you mention it," Marc said, "I am getting a little hungry. Must be all this salt air."

Once Jocelyn and Derek wandered off, an uncomfortable silence descended over the threesome. Picking up a handful of sand, Selena let it trickle through her fingers. Finally, Marc said, "So, where did Trevor and Amber get off to?"

Selena shrugged. "Who knows?"

"They went for a walk about half an hour ago," Lori said, digging around in her bag for a bottle of sunscreen.

As she slathered the warm lotion over her legs, Selena scooted closer to Marc. "Remember the time we camped out here and we . . . " she leaned over to whisper the rest in his ear.

A scarlet stain crept up Marc's neck. He jerked away from her touch. "I don't think now is the time to—"

"What's wrong?" Selena teased. "You didn't seem to mind then." She scooted behind him and began to massage his shoulders.

His face grew even redder. "Cut it out." When she refused to stop, he shook her off and stood up. "I think I'll go see if I can find Trevor and Amber. Be back later."

Selena snatched up her towel and beach bag. "I'll

just keep him company while he's searching for them."
"Good luck with that," Lori mumbled.

CHAPTER TWENTY-TWO

Once she'd finished slathering on sunscreen, Lori looked around for her beach bag, but couldn't find it. In her hurry to follow Marc, Selena must've grabbed the wrong bag. Oh, well. She tossed the bottle of sunscreen on the edge of her beach towel, then stretched out and closed her eyes. As she soaked up the sun's warmth, she listened to the soothing splash of waves against the boat and let her thoughts drift.

Half an hour passed before the others began to wander back. Trevor and Amber were the first to arrive, followed closely by Jocelyn and Derek. Marc trailed in some ten minutes later, minus Selena. They delayed lunch another thirty minutes waiting for Selena to straggle in, but finally gave up and ate without her.

By the time two o'clock rolled around, with still no sign of her, they began to worry. Dividing into teams—Trevor and Lori in one, Marc and Derek in another, with Jocelyn remaining behind with Amber—they set out to comb the island.

Fifteen minutes later, Trevor and Lori were the unlucky couple who found her. At first, Lori thought she must've fallen down, maybe twisted an ankle. Trevor called out to her, but she didn't answer.

He called her name again. She didn't move, or make any attempt to acknowledge their presence.

Trevor glanced at Lori, and they took off running.

As soon as they reached her, it was clear why Selena hadn't answered. There was a huge dent in the back of her head, as if someone had taken a bat to it. Her beautiful red hair had fallen out of its clip and was crusted with blood. Flies crawled over her body. And there was an odd, metal stench in the air.

All at once, bile catapulted up Lori's throat, setting off the gag reflex. She made it several feet away before throwing up the lunch she had just eaten. By then, the significance of what Selena was wearing seeped into her consciousness—a blue robe. *Her* blue robe. Suddenly her knees buckled, and she fell to the sand in a heap.

Had Annabel's premonition been wrong? Or should she be the one lying there?

Unmindful of the prickly spines of the cactus beside his daughter's body, Trevor knelt in the sand and felt for a pulse. After a moment, he pushed to his feet, his face grim. He didn't need to say the words aloud. They both knew Selena was dead.

Without speaking, Trevor pulled Lori to her feet and led her back to their picnic area. Derek and Marc were already there. Calling them over, he told them about Selena, then ordered Derek to take the women back to the marina and contact the police, while he and Marc went back to stand guard over the body.

Not up to facing Selena's Olds, they drove back to the house in Trevor's SUV. Lori ushered Amber upstairs and tried to keep her occupied with a game of monopoly.

That evening, there were questions to face: Who was the last person to see the victim alive? What kind of mood was she in? Where had each of them been around the time of her death?

When they were done, Lori headed upstairs, downed a couple of painkillers, and then crawled into bed fully clothed. Throughout the night, she was haunted by images of Selena's lifeless body. In her dreams, Marc stood over her body, a piece of driftwood clutched in his hand. With eyes glowing brightly, he turned to her and said, "I had to do it. She was evil. Everyone knew she wanted to hurt you."

It must have been around two when she woke up, drenched in sweat, wet clothes clinging to her body. Hoping to wash away all traces of her dream, she got up and took a shower. But no matter how hard she scrubbed, nothing could erase the memory of Marc saying, "I had to do it." The words kept looping through her mind.

She grabbed a soft, green towel and dried off. Then slipped on a fresh nightgown and headed into the bedroom to comb the tangles out of her hair. That's when she noticed the note tucked into the edge of the mirror. With a sense of dread, she reached for it. Written on plain, notebook paper, in bold, black letters, were the words: It should have been you.

The paper fell from her hand. She whirled around and swept the room for signs of an intruder, but saw no signs of one.

Still uneasy, she sprinted to the closet and flung open the door. There was no one hiding inside, ready to attack her in her sleep. She hustled over to the bed, dropped to the floor, and searched under the bed. It was clear, as well.

Recalling Derek's screwdriver trick, she checked the door. As far as she could tell, the lock hadn't been tampered with. Which meant, the note must have been placed on her dresser earlier that evening—before she'd come upstairs to get ready for bed.

She retrieved the note, then sagged down on the edge and read it again. This time, instead of fear, anger began to pulse through her veins. She was done being threatened. Another death had taken place. And this time the police had no choice but to call it murder.

CHAPTER TWENTY-THREE

As Lori dragged her weary limbs past the living room the next morning, Marc called out to her. Putting her need for caffeine on hold, she trudged back a few steps and leaned against the doorframe for support. Judging from the way he looked—eyes all red and bleary, clothes badly rumpled, stubble coating his face—he hadn't gotten any more sleep than she had.

"We need to talk," he said.

With remnants of her dream still fresh in her mind, she gave him a wary look and eased back a step. "About what?"

His eyes widened. "You can't actually believe that I killed Selena." He ran a hand through his hair. "She and I may have gotten into it from time to time, but I'd never . . . kill her. If I'd wanted to get rid of her, I would've simply divorced her."

She didn't like his choice of words—"get rid of her." It reminded her too much of her dream. As much as she wanted to believe in his innocence, she still harbored a few doubts. He *was* the last person to see Selena. And, despite Selena's claims that their marriage was in great shape, she knew that was far from the truth.

Before she could offer an explanation for her behavior, Trevor strolled out of the dining room and joined them. Unlike Marc, he was perfectly groomed in a dark, blue suit and red tie. "We need to talk about a few things before I clue Mother in on what's happened."

"Clue Mother in about what?" came Annabel's

chirpy voice from the foot of the stairs. Leaning heavily on her cane, she hobbled into the room. "Tell me what?" she repeated.

Today she looked more like her old self—vibrant, alive with curiosity. Dressed in another silk caftan, a beautiful turquoise this time, her hair was once again piled neatly atop her head, her makeup carefully applied.

"Why don't we sit down, Mother," Trevor said, taking her arm.

She refused to budge until she got some answers. "There's no need to coddle me, young man. Get on with what you have to say so we can have our breakfast and get to church. I'm feeling rather hungry this morning. I might even splurge and have one of those delicious cinnamon rolls Lou Ann made before she left."

"I would feel better if you'd sit down before we talk," Trevor said.

Pursing her lips, Annabel clamped on that I'm-the-mother-and-I'm-in-charge look, and waited.

"All right," he said, realizing he was beat. "I'm afraid I have some bad news about Selena."

Her shoulders sagged. "What has that child done now?"

"I'm afraid she's . . . she's . . . dead," he finally got the word out.

The color instantly drained from her face, and her body began to sway. Trevor reached out to steady her, and with Marc's help, got her to the sofa.

"I don't understand." She sounded bewildered. "When I saw her yesterday, she was fine. What happened?"

While Trevor recapped yesterday's events, Lori studied the frail woman. Something seemed off. Though Annabel mumbled all the usual clichés, Lori sensed she wasn't as broken up over Selena's death as she pretended to be. Then again, she might be hiding her feelings, hoping to spare her son more pain.

Before Lori had time to consider the impact her words might have, she blurted out, "First, Kay, now Selena. Who's next?"

All three turned to look at Lori.

Annabel was the first to speak. "She's right," she told Trevor. "Something has to be done. We can't allow this to go on any longer."

Allow what to go on? Lori wondered.

"Mother." Trevor knelt before her. "Don't upset yourself over this. Remember what the doctor said. You need to take it easy, keep your blood pressure under control. Let me handle this."

An understanding seemed to pass between mother and son. Annabel reached out and gave his hand a squeeze. "I know I can trust you to do what needs to be done."

"Not if he handles this like he did Kay's death," Lori muttered.

Marc laid a hand on her shoulder. "This is not the best time to get into that," he suggested softly. "Much as Annabel likes to pretend her health is fine, she hasn't been doing all that well these past few months."

Lori nodded, conceding his point. "You're right."

"If you gentlemen don't mind"—Annabel's gaze came to rest on Lori—"I'd like to speak with Lori alone."

Neither man seemed inclined to leave, but at Annabel's insistence they finally vacated the room. Don't upset her, Trevor's expression warned, as he shuffled past.

Once they were alone, Annabel patted the empty spot beside her. "Come over here and sit beside me, dear. I don't want to get a crick in my neck from looking up at you."

She wasn't entirely comfortable with her suggestion, but Lori padded across the room and sat down beside the older woman.

"What I'm going to say may sound rather harsh," Annabel warned, her eyes bright and probing.

Lori sat up straighter. "I can handle whatever you have to say without falling apart, if that's what you're worried about."

Satisfied with her answer, Annabel nodded. "Then I'll skip the social amenities and get right to the point. I don't mean to seem cruel, my dear, but somehow I think you're the cause of Selena's death. No—" She held up a hand forestalling any comment. "I don't mean that you actually killed her. I know you don't have a mean bone in your body. But I do think you were the intended target."

Her words didn't surprise Lori. For the past twelve hours, her thoughts had been running along the same line.

"I know you don't want to hear this," Annabel went on gently, "but I have to insist that you stop delving into Kay's death. It's not safe anymore. It appears, you've made an enemy. A dangerous enemy," she added.

The driving need to be understood propelled Lori off the sofa. "I can't do that." She stalked over to the fireplace, then whirled around to face Annabel, a look of regret on her face. "I'm sorry about Selena's death. More sorry than you can possibly know. But you have to understand . . . there's something inside me . . . pushing me . . . something that won't let me give up until I find out what happened to Kay."

Annabel shook her head and smiled sadly. "I was afraid of that." She seemed to deflate before Lori's eyes. The wrinkles in her face became deep crevices and her blue eyes seemed to fade to a clear crystal.

"Perhaps it's impossible to fight against the course of one's destiny anyway," she added, sounding like some new-age guru.

Lori didn't like the fatalistic sound of Annabel's words and suddenly felt an overwhelming desire to comfort her. She hurried back to the sofa, plopped down, and gave the older woman's shoulders a squeeze. The poor thing felt as fragile as a porcelain doll.

For a moment, Annabel clung to Lori. Then she disengaged herself, leaned back, and closed her eyes. "If you don't mind, dear, I'm feeling rather tired. Why don't you run along now. I think I'll sit here and rest awhile."

"Would you like me to—"

"I'll be fine. Run along now and have your breakfast."

Instead of heading into the dining room where she'd have to deal with Trevor and Marc, Lori ducked out the front door. It was still early in the day, the sun low in the sky. Dew clung to the grass and foliage. She slipped around the side of the house and sat down at one of the tables on the patio, wanting to mull over what Annabel had said about not being able to change the course of one's destiny.

What if her destiny led her down the same path as Selena's had?

She didn't want to die. She hadn't done anything important with her life yet. She wanted to live to be an old woman, surrounded by a husband, and kids, and grandkids.

Her attempt to hide didn't last long. Marc came around the corner of the house and joined her. "I thought I might find you here," he said, and collapsed in the chair beside her.

Before he could say anymore, she began a non-stop monologue about her life in Texas. When her stream of words finally dried up, Marc zeroed in on the question she was hoping to avoid, "What did Annabel want?"

She thought about making something up, but realized she might as well get it over with. "To tell me it's my fault Selena is dead."

Eyes widening, he jerked back in his chair. "That's absurd."

She shook her head. "Not really. If I hadn't been so intent on finding out who killed Kay then—"

He threw up a hand. "Don't go there. Selena's death was not your fault. Chances are, the two deaths aren't even related."

At her skeptical look, he changed tactics. "Even if they are connected, it doesn't mean anything. Have you given any thought to the idea that maybe Selena's known all along who killed Kay? And maybe that person killed her to insure her silence?"

Lori knew he was trying to make her feel better and appreciated the effort. Some part of her longed to cling to him, after all, Selena's death had left him a free man. Yet, at the same time, her death had driven a wedge between them that could never be bridged.

He must have read her mind. "Someday we'll be able to put all this behind us and get on with our lives."

"Will we?" She gazed into those intense, gray eyes.

"I'm sure of it," he said quietly.

Was he right? Would they someday be free of Selena, or would her death forever haunt them?

Intent on each other, neither heard Seth's approach. "Hmm," he cleared his throat.

Marc glanced up. "What can we do for you, Seth?"

"Nothing you can do," Seth said, "but if it's all right, I'd like to have a word with the young lady."

Lori stood up. "Of course, you may have a word with me. And you don't need anyone's permission to do so but my own."

Seth's attention shifted back to Lori. He nodded, then led her across the damp grass to a clump of azaleas. Standing there in his wrinkled overalls, white prickles of hair covering his chin, he looked older, as if the last few days had accelerated the aging process. "I reckon, I best get right to the point." He hesitated a moment, studying her reaction.

At her nod, he pressed on. "I came to find out what you know about my grandbaby's death," he laid it out bluntly.

For a moment, Lori was at a loss. "Surely, Trevor, or Jocelyn told you what happened."

He nodded. "My daughter told me, but she was rantin' and ravin' about so many things, I don't rightly know what to think."

Or who to blame.

She filled him in on what she knew, leaving him free to draw his own conclusion. He listened without interrupting, and when she was done, said, "Well, I appreciate you taking the time to tell me all this." Unshed tears made his eyes glisten. "I reckon I best be getting back to work now."

As he turned to go, Lori said, "I'm very sorry for your loss."

"Time's gone for being sorry," he muttered. "Time now to make whoever did this terrible thing pay for what he's done. Won't be no more covering up like before." He trotted off in the direction of his house and was soon swallowed up by a jungle of shrubbery.

This cover-up he'd alluded to, could it have something to do with Kay's death? Or was he referring to an incident further in the past—say, around the time Jocelyn had been kicked out of Oakwood and the black sheep of the family had taken off for parts unknown?

CHAPTER TWENTY-FOUR

The rest of the day seemed to plod by. Trevor spent most of his time locked in his study. Annabel kept Amber occupied upstairs, while Marc and Jocelyn headed off to take care of funeral arrangements. Derek didn't appear all day, leaving Lori free to wander aimlessly about the house, unable to settle in any one place.

By nightfall, some of the neighbors began to arrive with offerings of food, though none of them seemed to have any appetite. It was well after midnight when Lori finally plodded upstairs. Before climbing under the covers, she opened a window and found the night air alive with music: crickets chirping, frogs croaking—off in the distance, the whistle of a train. Across the lawn, the moon cast a soft, almost magical glow.

As she watched shadows dance across the yard, a light went on in Selena's workshop. At first, she thought her imagination was playing tricks on her. But when she closed her eyes and reopened them, the light was still there.

Someone was skulking around in Selena's workshop.

Realizing she'd never be able to sleep until she knew who was there, she slipped on her robe and house slippers, grabbed the flashlight from her nightstand, and headed downstairs. As she crept through the silent house, a warning message flickered through her brain, but she brushed it aside, promised herself she would only take a quick peek, then hightail it back inside. No loitering. No barging inside. No confronting any intruder.

She left the door open a crack in case she needed to make a hasty retreat. As she stole through the yard, the moonlight made the flashlight unnecessary. She was almost to the shed when she heard breaking glass. Throwing caution to the wind, she sprinted to the window and peered inside.

And jerked back when a piece of pottery sailed toward her and smashed into the potter's wheel beneath the window.

For a few minutes, all was quite. She eased up and peered inside again. Saw Jocelyn hunched over Selena's workbench. She wasn't sure whether to be relieved, or to send her feet flying back to the safety of the house.

As she debated the matter, Jocelyn must have caught sight of her because she snatched a plate off one of the bookshelves and yelled, "Go away!" Then sent it soaring toward the window.

Acting on instinct, Lori crouched down, moments before a plate hit the newly replaced windowpane. Shards of glass rained down around her, forcing her to abandon her no-confrontation plan and storm inside.

"Why don't you tell me what's bothering you, Jocelyn," she said, "before you ruin all of Selena's work. Maybe I can help."

"Talking to you isn't going to bring my baby back." Jocelyn slid around the workbench and disappeared from sight.

Staying low, Lori inched forward, stepping around shards of broken pottery. A soft, whimpering noise came from someplace near the back wall. She quickened her step, rounded the corner, and found Jocelyn slumped in the corner. "Are you hurt? Should I call for help?"

The self-assured woman she'd met a few days ago was gone. Tonight, those exotic green eyes were devoid of make-up, her eyelids swollen from crying. Her thick, red mane, so sleek and shiny when they'd met, had become nothing but a frizzy halo.

Hunkering down beside her, Lori said, "What are you doing out here so late?"

Without offering any explanation, Jocelyn sagged against the wall.

"I know you're upset about what happened to Selena," Lori said. "We all are. But all this drama isn't going to bring her back."

Jocelyn pushed away from the wall and stood up. "How dare you talk to me like that."

"I didn't mean to hurt your feelings," Lori said, getting to her feet.

The fire died in those cat green eyes. "It's just that . . . I feel so helpless. She was my baby and I didn't protect her."

Lori sucked in a breath. Ever since Kay's death she herself had lived with those same feelings, reliving all the times she should've been there for Kay and wasn't. "I know how you feel. I—"

Before she could finish her thought, Jocelyn snapped out, "You have no idea how I feel. There was nothing you could've done to save your sister, but me, I could've saved my baby."

As Jocelyn's words penetrated her sleep deprived brain, Lori rocked back on her heels. "You know who killed them, don't you?"

"Don't be ridiculous. The police already ruled your sister's death an accident. And my baby's death was nothing but a random act of violence committed by some stranger."

There was something in her voice that made Lori press on. "You're lying. You know who did this. You know who killed Kay and Selena."

Jocelyn scooted over to the workbench and plopped down on a stool. "Don't be ridiculous. I'm a stranger here. I've only been back in town a few weeks. I haven't the slightest idea what's going on in this godforsaken town."

Determined to get to the truth, Lori planted herself in front of the workbench. "Who killed them?"

Jocelyn fiddled with the modeling tool Selena had been using last time they were here. "I have no idea."

Lori studied her through narrowed eyes. "I can understand why you wouldn't care about finding Kay's killer, but I can't believe you'd stand by and let someone get away with murdering your own child. No one could be that heartless."

Jocelyn opened her mouth to reply, then went still, her gaze riveted on something behind Lori's shoulder.

When she swung around, Derek was standing in the doorway, watching them. There was no glint of laughter in his eyes, only a bone chilling anger. He gave a deep sigh, then stepped across the threshold and closed the door behind him. All six feet of rugged muscle moved in her direction. "You couldn't leave things alone, could you?" There was no trace of warmth in his voice. "You had to keep digging for answers. No matter who got hurt."

The smell of fear oozed from Lori's pores. Her temples pounded. And her heart began to throb painfully. She stumbled back and crashed into the hard surface of the workbench.

While Derek's attention was focused on her, Jocelyn tried to scoot past him. But he was too fast for her. He grabbed her arm and flung her into the workbench as if she were nothing more than a rag doll. There was a cracking sound as her head slammed into solid wood. She groaned once, then slumped to the floor.

His attention turned back to Lori. "You really want to know who killed Selena? I'll tell you who killed her. You did. With all those stupid questions of yours."

"You can't blame me for what happened to her. I wasn't the one who bashed in her head."

"Shut up!" he yelled.

Until she came up with a better plan, she decided to humor him.

"Good girl," he said, when he realized she was complying with his request. He smiled, but there was no warmth in his eyes. They remained cold, hard, unforgiving.

"It was all your meddling that turned Selena against me. When she found out what I did to Kay, she threatened to go to the police. Of course, I couldn't allow that. You understand that, right?" From the matter-of-fact way he spoke, she knew he had passed through the threshold of sanity into the world of madness.

"You . . . you killed Kay?" The words came from her mouth, but sounded far away.

Pleased by her reaction, he grinned. "You never guessed, did you? I didn't think so."

"But you were out of town when Kay died. In D.C."

"That's what everyone thought. Truth was, I was staying at a little motel outside of Jackson."

"What did Kay do to make you hate her so much?"

"Oh, it had nothing to do with hating Kay. In fact, I rather liked her. She was a sweet girl, really."

She shook her head, feeling confused. "Let me get this straight. You liked Kay, thought she was a sweet girl, yet you killed her. That doesn't make any sense."

"It does when you consider how much Trevor loved her." A smiled touched his lips. "How much he suffered when I took her away from him."

"But . . . he's your brother."

"And he needed to pay for all the pain he has caused me. And with more than a few lousy dollars."

The pieces began to fall into place. "You were in on the blackmail scheme with Jocelyn."

He seemed pleased with himself. "It was my idea."

"But the baby Kay was carrying . . . "

He laughed harshly. "Why should I care about his majesty's son. The one he'd someday pass the reins of *our* father's company to. He was nothing more than another obstacle to rob me of what's rightfully mine."

"Son?" Lori repeated. "She was having a boy?"

"You didn't know?" His eyebrows spiked up. "That's right. I remember now. Kay wanted to wait until she was further along to tell you. Said, she wanted it to be a surprise."

She tamped down her fear. "But it would've been years before he was old enough to take over the company. Which he might not even want to."

He pinched the space between his eyes. "No more talk about the baby. Trevor took my child from me. Why shouldn't I take his?"

She shook her head in confusion. "Your child."

"Don't tell me you haven't figured out the family secret."

The truth hit her like a bolt of lightning. "Selena is your daughter, not Trevor's. But how is that possible? Trevor and Jocelyn were practically newlyweds when Selena was born."

Of course, it would explain a few things. Like: Why Trevor had so little affection for his first-born daughter. And why he had such contempt for his only sibling.

"Jocelyn was already pregnant with my child when Trevor married her," he was delighted to explain. "When the baby arrived a bit . . . prematurely . . . it didn't take him long to figure out who the baby's father was. I decided to disappear for awhile, give him time to cool down."

"If Jocelyn was carrying your baby, why didn't you marry her?"

"Because I wasn't ready to settle down. Besides, Trevor was the one who inherited our father's business and Oakwood. How could I compete with that?"

"But if Jocelyn loved you . . . "

"It was always about money with Jocelyn," he said. "She would never have given up being mistress of Oakwood to live in an apartment with me."

His words matched her assessment of Jocelyn. "If Trevor knew the baby wasn't his, then why did he keep Selena? Why not send her away with her mother?"

He quirked up an eyebrow. "And lose his hold over me?"

"Surely Seth, or Annabel wouldn't let him get away with that."

He snorted. "Don't kid yourself. Neither one of them had the guts to cross Trevor." He paused, then went on, as if he wanted her to understand, "All my life, I've had to live in Trevor's shadow. He was the golden son. The one who could do no wrong in the old man's eyes. I, on the other hand, might as well have been invisible. You know"—his voice faltered—"the old man never once asked me to go fishing with the two of them. He never came to any of my football games. Yet when Trevor—" he broke off, overcome with emotion.

"I'm sure your father loved both of you," she said, trying to keep him talking until she came up with a plan. "Maybe he just had more in common with Trevor."

"No," he snapped. "I've never kidded myself. It was Trevor he loved. Trevor he worshiped. I don't think he even realized he had two sons. But in the end, he paid for that mistake." A self-satisfied glow lit his eyes, turning them into chunks of gleaming crystal. "Yes, indeed. I'd say he paid for that mistake quite dearly."

"How did he pay?" she felt compelled to ask, but feared she already knew the answer.

That terrifying smile was back. "How else? With his life."

"You were just a boy when your father died. You couldn't have—"

"Killed him?" he completed her thought. "It was simple really. It had been raining heavily the day of his accident. The roads were slick. Everyone knew the old man always drove too fast. So I merely put his love to the test."

Coldness began to seep through her body and settle around her heart. "How?" she asked, her voice barely audible.

"It was easy. I put on one of Trevor's old fishing outfits and waited by the side of the road. When the old man came flying around dead man's curve and saw his beloved son step into the road, he had a choice to make: ram into his precious son, or swerve into a stand of pines and take his chances."

"Of course, being the perfect father, he chose to save his son's life." As almost an after thought, he added, "I always wondered if he would have made the same choice if he'd known it was me standing there that day."

CHAPTER TWENTY-FIVE

Derek had killed too many times to alter his pattern now. Lori's only chance for survival was to keep him talking and hope help arrived. "What about Annabel?" She spit out the first idea that came to mind. "Does she know you killed her husband and granddaughter?"

He shrugged. "She has her suspicions, but, unlike the old man, I was always her favorite. Actually, she's the reason I'm here now. After her health problems last year, she made Trevor send for me."

"Annabel doesn't have a mean bone in her body. I can't believe she would stand by and let you get away with murder."

"What can I say?" He shrugged. "She loves me."

Lori knew there was nothing stronger than the love a mother had for her child, but to stand by while he murdered innocent people . . . She didn't understand how Annabel could live with herself. "So breaking into my room, the ordeal in the attic, the note on my dresser—you were responsible for all those things?"

He nodded. "Too bad you didn't heed my warning and leave while you had the chance." He reached behind his back, pulled a gun from the waistband of his jeans, then motioned toward the door. "You and I are going for a little walk."

"You'll never get away with this." Panic sent her voice ratcheting up a notch. "Three deaths in a row. The police aren't going to buy another accident. And what about Jocelyn, are you planning to kill her too?"

"I've already taken care of that problem," he said.

"A wife can't be forced to testify against her husband."

Her mouth sagged open in surprise.

He gave a mirthless laugh. "You could say Jocelyn and I have been living off Trevor's generosity for quite some time. Not that he realizes it, of course."

"You haven't thought this through," she said. "Nobody's going to believe—"

He cut her off. "You'd be surprised what people will believe. When Jocelyn wakes up, I suspect her story is going to go something like this: She saw a light on in Selena's workshop, went to investigate, and found you trashing the place. When she confronted you, you admitted that you killed Selena because she was responsible for your sister's death."

Hoping reason might prevail, Lori said, "Aren't you forgetting something? The police already ruled Kay's death an accident."

He grinned. "Too bad they were mistaken. Those dolls on the stairs were a nice touch, don't you think? I figured the police would blame the kid for your sister's death. I hadn't counted on Trevor putting them back in Amber's room. Guess he didn't want anybody blaming his precious, little girl for her mother's death."

Anger pumped through Lori's veins. "Yet, Selena did blame her."

He shrugged. "I suppose it's understandable. Daddy's little girl got all the attention. There wasn't much love left over for Selena."

"That's no excuse for hurting a child," she said. "For making her feel responsible for her mother's death. No decent human being would do that to an innocent child."

He shrugged. "Selena had ever right to resent her little sister. Just like she resented you—the woman who stole her husband's love."

"I'm not a husband stealer," Lori said. "What Marc

and I had was over a long time ago. I don't know why Selena couldn't get that through her thick head."

"Probably because it wasn't over."

She opened her mouth, ready to dispute his claim, then realized it didn't matter. In a short time her life would be over. Who she loved, or didn't love wasn't going to matter."

"Now, where was I?" He thought about it a moment, then returned to his scenario. "Oh yeah, you couldn't live with the guilt of taking another person's life. Even if they deserved it. So you waved the gun around you took from Trevor's desk and threatened to kill yourself. Jocelyn tried to stop you, but you shoved her into Selena's workbench and she was knocked unconscious." He paused, his lips thinning into a smile. "How am I doing so far?"

Not too bad.

"There's one problem with your little scenario—I would never kill myself. No matter how depressed I got. That's what antidepressants are for."

His eyebrows arched up. "Really?" He studied her. "You look pretty depressed to me. I think, when your body is found on the beach in the morning, I can convince the authorities that you committed suicide. You see, officers, she was so distraught over her sister's death . . . and with what she did to Selena . . . "

"No one will believe I killed Selena. As for killing myself with that thing"—she gestured at the weapon he was holding—"I hate guns. I've never even held one in my hand, much less fired one."

"Oh, they'll believe you killed Selena, all right. Not only did she murder your sister, but she also stole the man you loved."

Lori gave a snort. "Like I told you, there hasn't been anything between the two of us in ages."

He rolled his eyes. "Anyone with half a brain can tell

there's something going on between you two."

"The only thing going on between us is looking into my sister's murder."

"If you say so." He waved the gun toward the door. "Time to get moving."

She saw no other option but to comply. Since she was no longer in possession of her flashlight, she was forced to stumble along, with only moonlight to brighten her path. She fell down once, only to be jerked to her feet by the collar of her robe. "Don't even think about playing games with me," Derek said, and jabbed the gun into her side, "or I'll kill you right here." He gave her a push with the heel of his hand.

As they resumed their march to the beach, she finally accepted the fact no one was coming to her rescue. Her mind scrambled for a plan of escape, but with the gun only inches from her back, any action she took would likely get her killed.

Once they reached the beach, she realized she had nothing more to lose. Whether she acted or not, her life would be over in a matter of minutes. Better to die fighting than to plod along like some dumb animal being led to the slaughter.

She faked a stumble and cried out, "My ankle. I think I sprained it." Doubling over, she pretended to check for damage.

Derek prodded her with his foot. "A sprained ankle is the least of your problems. Now, get moving."

It was now, or never. In one fluid motion, she grabbed a handful of sand, straightened, and flung the gritty particles into Derek's face. He reacted just the way she expected, he snapped his eyes shut and threw up his hands in a defensive gesture. Taking advantage of his temporary blindness, she moved in and jammed her knee into his groin.

He screamed in pain and went down on one knee.

Nobody's fool, she took off running.

Behind her, she heard Derek swear, get to feet, and stumble after her. Knowing his injury wouldn't slow him down long, she cut across the beach and dove into the woods, hoping it would provide some much-needed cover.

The dense canopy of leaves overhead allowed little moonlight to seep through, making it hard to see. Nevertheless, she plunged through the undergrowth like a wild animal. Branches and vines tore at her skin. Ignoring the discomfort, she worked her way toward Seth's house, hoping he knew how to use that rifle hanging on his dining room wall.

Before long, her chest began to ache with the effort of breathing. Her calves, not used to all this running, began to burn. The crunch of leaves behind her sent a surge of adrenaline pouring into her veins, which made her legs pump harder.

Seth's cabin finally sprang into view. His porch light glowed brightly, beaming a welcome. She opened her mouth to scream for help, but nothing came out. Before she could make another attempt, Derek lurched out of the darkness, grabbed hold of her hair, and yanked her against his chest.

A soft, whimpering noise escaped her mouth, as tears pooled down her cheeks.

"You're going to pay for that little prank." He gave her hair another yank, cocked the gun, and shoved it against the side of her head. He pulled the trigger and—click. "Gotcha," he said, and smiled sadistically.

She was so cold her teeth began to chatter.

"How about the next chamber," he said. "Shall we see if there's a bullet in it?"

He forced the gun into her right hand and clamped his hand over hers. With his superior strength, he had no problem forcing the barrel toward her mouth. She did everything she could to escape his grasp. She stomped on his foot, kicked at his shins. But nothing worked.

As the gun inched closer to her mouth, bone chilling laughter began to spill from Derek's mouth. The hair on the back of her neck stood up. "You don't have to do this," she pleaded. "I promise I won't tell anyone what you did."

"It's too late for promises. I tried to warn you. But you had keep sticking your nose into things that didn't concern you."

From the corner of her eye, Lori saw Seth step out from a clump of bushes. "Let the girl go," he yelled, shifting his rife into firing position.

For an instant, Derek froze. Then he jerked the gun from Lori's hand, whirled around, and fired.

The bullet tore through Seth's shoulder. He grunted and went down on one knee. Then fell, face first, into the dirt.

Realizing she needed to draw Derek's attention away from the injured man, Lori took off running. A bullet zipped past her left ear and hit the tree in front of her. She crouched, shifted to the right, and kept on moving.

The deeper into the woods she went, the soggier the ground became. Mud sucked at her slippers. She tripped and stumbled a few times, but summoned the strength to keep going.

With his longer legs, Derek was catching up fast.

Another shot whizzed through the air and tore into her left shoulder. Hot, burning fire sizzled through her body. She fell to her knees, sucked in a breath, and prayed for the pain to end.

She had to get moving before Derek could get off another shot. Supporting her injured arm with her right hand, she pushed to her feet and slid behind the nearest tree. As she leaned against the rough bark, blood seeped through her fingers and pooled in the bend of her arm.

"You might as well give up now," Derek said. "You won't get far with that injury."

"It's just a flesh wound," Lori lied, trying to keep her voice steady.

"I'll make it quick," he promised. "You won't suffer."

How stupid did he think she was? "You'll never get away with your suicide story now. The cops will know I was shot from behind."

"So, I'll come up with a new story. I have a pretty good imagination. I'm sure I can come up with something they'll believe."

"What about Seth?" she started to say, but caught herself in time. Better keep his attention focused on her.

The snap of a twig warned her Derek was on the move. She had no choice but to keep going. She pushed away from the massive trunk, crouched, then aimed for another tree several yards away.

"Come out, come out, wherever you are," Derek called softly, moving straight toward her.

She pressed a hand against her shoulder to stem the flow of blood and ran, using the trees for cover, circling back toward Seth's house. She prayed that he was still alive, had somehow managed to call for help.

Ahead, she heard a branch snap and dropped to her knees. Had Derek managed to get in front of her? She squatted there, motionless, eyes trained on the spot where she thought the sound had come from.

Slowly, her vision began to blur, making her feel a bit woozy, like a dense fog was creeping into her brain. She shook her head, trying to clear it. She couldn't be sure, but she thought she saw someone moving her way.

Out of the mist, Marc's face appeared. "Thank God you're alive." He bent down and caressed her face.

She wanted to fall into his arms, cling to him, and never let go. But she was too tired to move.

Another voice, cut through the fog. "This must be my lucky night." Derek stepped into view. "I suppose, I'll have to make a few adjustments to my plan. How does this sound? Step-sister of Selena Towell killed when she accuses husband of murder? Husband kills himself in remorse?" Raising the gun, he took aim at Lori's head.

"No!" Marc yelled, launching himself on top of her.

The shot whizzed by, missing them by mere inches, and plowed into the tree behind them.

Before Derek could get off another round, Trevor tore out of the woods, carrying Seth's rifle. Without hesitating, he took aim and fired.

The bullet slammed into Derek's back. He swayed, half turned, and slowly fell to the ground.

He didn't move. Not even when Trevor prodded him with his foot.

Derek Grant, my sister's killer, was dead.

CHAPTER TWENTY-SIX
One Year Later

Lori was putting away her camera equipment when the bell over the door of her studio pealed. "Sorry, we're closed," she called out as she emerged from the back room. "If you'd like to schedule an appointment–" she broke off when she saw who was standing there. "Marc!" She shook her head, wondering if she was dreaming. "What on earth are you doing here?"

Sauntering over to the counter, he said, "Thought I'd check out the job market in this part of the country."

Her brow knotted. "What about the Silver Sands?" A thought pushed into her mind. "You didn't lose your business, I hope. Not over all that stuff with Derek."

"Nothing like that," he quickly assured her. "It's just that . . . well . . . I sold the place two weeks ago and—"

She frowned. "But the restaurant was your dream."

"Dreams change. Besides, ever since . . . you know," he said, not willing to put into words the horror they'd gone through a year ago, "it hasn't been the same."

She nodded. Multiple homicides weren't something you got over quickly—if ever.

"It got so that every time I walked past the spot where Selena's Corner had been, all the memories came flooding back. I decided it was time to make a fresh start somewhere else. And Texas seemed as good a place as any."

She knew what he meant about memories flooding back. She still had nightmares about being chased through the woods by a homicidal maniac. But she refused to dwell on it. "How's the rest of the family?"

"Okay, I guess. Six months ago, Trevor sold his business, put Oakwood on the market, and moved the family to California."

Her eyes widened. "I can't believe he'd sell Oakwood. It's been in his family for ages. His great-grandfather built the place."

"Yeah, well," he shrugged, "I guess he has his own demons to battle."

"What about Seth and Jocelyn?"

"Currently, enjoying the sunny beaches of Florida." He shook his head. "But I didn't come here to talk about them." He hesitated. "I don't know how you feel about us after what happened, but I thought we might spend some time together, get to know each other again."

She studied his face. Was she ready to open her heart to this man? Could she trust him not to shatter it? Memories began to flood through her mind. Derek aiming his gun at her. Marc throwing his body over hers, protecting her from harm.

Maybe she'd spent enough time in the shadow of death. It was time to step into the light and live again.

A feeling of peace settled over her. She smiled. "Buy me a cup of coffee and we'll talk about it."

His eyes twinkled. "Babe, if you play your cards right, I'll even toss in a slice of apple pie to sweeten the deal."

She grinned. "On second thought, maybe I'd better pay for the pie, since you're unemployed at the moment."

"Oh, you'll pay all right." He came around the counter and pulled her into his arms. "I'll see to that."

The End

ABOUT THE AUTHOR

 **Teresa LaRue** grew up in a small town along the Mississippi Gulf Coast. She's worked as a secretary, assistant manager of an audio book store, and manager of a fashion jewelry store. She is an avid reader, gardener, and movie buff. She lives across the lake from New Orleans with her family, including a dog named Bones, and a cat named Chloe.

www.ingramcontent.com/pod-product-compliance
Lightning Source LLC
Chambersburg PA
CBHW031308120626
46554CB00001BA/336